D0528360

Death at the Theatre

MISS HART AND MISS HUNTER
INVESTIGATE BOOK 2

Celina Grace

This book is for my aunt,
Rosemary Farley, with love.

Author's Note:

THIS BOOK IS WRITTEN IN British English. Therefore some spellings, grammar usage and sentence construction might differ from standard American usage (e.g. 'realise' rather than 'realize').

Chapter One

I SAW IT AS SOON AS I came up the steps at Oxford Circus. The words were there, booming black on still-white paper; the glaring headlines, the name that had been on everyone's lips for the last three weeks. Even if I'd been suddenly struck blind I wouldn't have been able to escape it: the paperboys were calling out the headlines in those half-musical tones that rang out like the cries of a strange bird.

"Lord Cartwright acquitted! Lord C found not guilty! Get your Evening Standard here-yah!"

I froze, right on the steps, and someone cannoned into me from the back and tutted, and I staggered a little in my one pair of good shoes, which had heels slightly higher than I was used to. Someone grabbed me under the arm as I started to fall. They righted me and were gone before I had a chance to thank them – indeed, I just about realised they were young and male before they were lost in the crowd. More than a little shaken, I limped up the rest of the steps, going with the streaming crowd, and approached the newsstand. I fumbled in my bag for a coin and took up the evening newspaper with trembling hands.

It was impossible to try and read it standing there. I hurried into the relative shelter of an office doorway and then realised I had no time to stand and read, even though I wanted to. I bundled the paper under one arm, hiding those shouting black headlines, and began to walk quickly down Great Regent's Street.

As I scurried along, my feet aching in the unaccustomed shoes, my mind flew from one person to another, wondering whether they knew and what their reaction would be to the news. Inspector Marks, Gladys, Dorothy, Mrs Anstells, Mrs Watling and – just as I rounded the corner to see her standing outside the Connault theatre, almost hopping from one foot to another in an fever of impatience – Verity. Of course.

"Where have you *been*?" she said in an agonised tone as I hurried up to her. "The second bell's about to go. Come on, come on, I've got your ticket, let's go, go, go!"

I didn't have time to tell her about that evening's news. I didn't have time to tell her anything at all. She grabbed my arm and whisked me through the theatre reception area, waving the tickets at the man standing by the foot of the stairs. "Sorry, Harry, she's just turned up, we'll go straight on up," Verity said and pulled me bodily up the stairs.

"Where are we sitting?" I panted as we rocketed past the entrance to the Dress Circle.

Verity gave me a wry look over her shoulder as she steamed ahead of me. "Gods, Joanie, where else? Free tickets though, so we can't complain."

I didn't have enough breath in me to complain. We eventually found our row and stumbled through the darkness to our seats, falling into them in a breathless tumble fortunately mostly right side up. Luckily our seats were towards the end of the row, near the entrance.

Giggling, Verity and I subsided, trying to control our breathing. There were a few irritated glances and tuts from the few people around us, but this was the Gods, after all – people didn't expect much. They weren't bad seats, apart from being high enough to give you vertigo. I leant forward, carefully, and looked at the stage, the boxes either side, the curtain which seemed to quiver in anticipation and felt a surge of excitement. I loved the theatre. I loved everything about it.

We didn't have drinks, or a programme, or opera glasses or anything like that, of course. I didn't care. Under cover of darkness, just as the orchestra struck up, I shrugged off my coat and leant back against the red velvet of my seat. I felt Verity grab my hand and squeeze it as the curtain went up, and the lights began to come up over the stage. I threw her a grateful grin – she was the one who'd organised these tickets, after all; her uncle, Tommy, was in the play. As I looked over her way, I could see we weren't the only late comers. A woman was fumbling her way towards a seat a few chairs along from us. It was too dark to see much – I could only see the curve of her cloche hat and the gleam of some sort of jewellery around her throat. I squeezed Verity's hand back, as a sort of thank you, and turned my attention towards the stage.

It was a very thrilling play. Caroline Carpenter played the lead role, that of a missionary torn between the love of two men and her religious calling. I'd seen Miss Carpenter once before, and she'd been so good that it was mostly the idea of seeing her act again that had made me want to see the play. She was very beautiful, with a kind of languid grace that gradually tightened into a marvellous taut intensity as the emotional tempo of the scene grew. Tommy, Verity's uncle, was playing against type as the 'bad boy', the lover who would only be bad for her. Knowing Tommy as I did, it should have been quite comical to see him stalking about the stage, his red hair dyed black and a thin black moustache shadowing his sneering lips. But Tommy was gifted too and he made it seem natural. The leading man, Aldous Smith, was new to me. He was good too, not quite as talented as Caroline and Tommy but certainly watchable, not least because he was almost as pretty as Caroline Carpenter.

Breathlessly, I watched as the drama unfolded before my eyes. I'd reached that happy state where I was so engrossed I had almost forgotten I was at the theatre – instead I was there, with the actors, on the deck of a cruise ship sailing for Africa. I was almost unaware of Verity sitting beside me, of the musty smell of the worn red velvet of the theatre seats, of the fact that I was surrounded by hundreds of people, sitting around me, and beneath me, in the dark, equally engrossed.

The final scene of the first act wound to its dramatic conclusion, with the lady missionary looking as though she was going to succumb to the charms of the dastardly adventurer. A moment of ringing silence fell across the stage just before the curtain came down. After another moment of silence in the dark, the theatre exploded with applause. The lights came on, strong enough to make you blink, and then it was as though reality rushed back in to fill the gap.

I sat back in my seat and blew out my cheeks, looking over at Verity. She had a starriness to her gaze that I knew I would see in my own eyes if I had a mirror handy – the look of someone coming back to Earth after an hour of transportation into another realm.

"Golly," Verity said, smiling. "What a dramatic play. Isn't Tommy good?"

"He's wonderful," I agreed. It was only then I realised how hot it was up in the Gods. I unbuttoned my cardigan and slipped it from my shoulders. "Shall we get a quick breath of air in the interval? Or stay here?"

Verity was saved from replying by a minor kerfuffle occurring in the row of seats in front of us. Apparently a man was seated at the end of the row, blocking access for the four increasingly irritated people who were trying to get past.

"I say, do you think you could move and let us past?" one of the women said in an increasingly vexed tone. The man at the end of the row took no notice. He was sitting with a hat pulled down over his eyes, and it was difficult to see his face.

I don't know what made me take a second, sharper look at him. His stillness, perhaps, or the way his head was leaning to one side against the back of the seat. I was just opening my mouth to say something – I'm not sure what – when one of the men in the group before us leant down and shook the man by the shoulder. The two women made noises between gasps and squeaks, but the man doing the shaking took no notice. He was a stout fellow wearing a rather dusty-looking topper. I hoped he'd removed it for the performance.

"Bally fellow's out of his mind with drink," he said and shook the man again, harder this time.

I moved forward, one hand on Verity to bring her with me, but by that time, it was too late. The body of the man in the end row seat fell sideways, and we all saw the scarlet mess that was his shirt-front. There was a moment of silence to equal that of the one heard at the end of the first act, and then the screams began, as loud and emphatic as those of an opera singer.

Chapter Two

THE POLICE SEEMED TO TAKE an absolute age to arrive but I suppose they didn't really – it just felt like that. As soon as the shock of confronting the body had worn off, Verity had raced off to find the manager of the theatre – she knew him slightly, through Tommy – and it was left to me to try and restore some order in the Gods. I don't think I did a very good job.

"Who on Earth do you think you are, miss?" cried the stout gentlemen as I suggested that we all take some seats over in the far corner to wait for the arrival of the police. One of the women, the one who'd first asked the dead man to move, was having hysterics and I could see her friend wasn't far behind her.

I don't know what imp of mischief made me say it. Perhaps it was because I was in the theatre – perhaps some spirit of drama that inhabited these four walls made me do it.

"I *am* the police," I said, sternly. I made my voice

go as steely and as upper class as possible – it was easy, I'd heard Verity do it many times, always to good effect. "Undercover. The uniformed officers will be here soon so I suggest we all move away from the body and wait for them to get here. Sir, if you would?"

Tophat's eyes bulged. I'm not sure he believed me but he wasn't quite so sure of himself as to question me, just in case I was telling the truth. The two women were too busy having the vapours to take much notice. Somehow, I got them to move back three rows, and we stood in the aisle in a crowded and awkward group. We were the only people up here, I realised. Had there been any others and had they left by a different exit? Ignoring Tophat's huffing and puffing beside me, I looked around this level of the theatre. There was only one entrance and exit, the door beyond the dead man. It was then I remembered the woman who had come in late, even after Verity and I. She wasn't here now. Had she left just before the discovery of the body? I racked my memory, trying to see if I could recall her, but it was hopeless. I had no recollection of her movements whatsoever.

I left my little group of indignant and weeping theatre-goers and walked towards the body. I didn't get too close – I knew I shouldn't touch anything. But shouldn't I at least check to make sure he was dead? What if he wasn't, despite the wounds in

11

his chest? It was hard to see his face, due to the flat cap pulled down over his brow, but he looked fairly young. He was clean-shaven but for a thin moustache. I looked at what he was wearing – nondescript men's clothing, fairly worn looking. I tried to keep my eyes from the bloody mess that was the front of his chest. It looked as though he'd been stabbed. Quickly, before I could think twice, I pressed my fingers to his neck.

The coolness of the skin beneath my fingertips told me the truth. No pulse, however weak and faint, beat beneath my hand. Nodding to myself, I moved backwards. Well, at least I knew now that the poor man was beyond help. My eyes dropped again to the stab wounds and the bloom of blood that surrounded each one.

I moved back a row, so I could see the back of his chair. I drew in my breath. There were two slits in the fabric of the chair, both stained with blood. Someone had obviously sat behind him and thrust a knife through the back of the seat. I stared at the holes in the velvet and repressed a shiver. There was something so dreadfully cold-hearted about the thought. Someone had quite literally stabbed him in the back.

At that moment, Verity came through the doorway, panting and scarlet-faced. She hurried over to me. "The police will be here very shortly. David is on his way up."

"David?" I asked.

"The theatre manager. Be warned, he's in quite a taking."

"I'm not surprised." I drew Verity away from the body, back towards the little group of people in the far aisle. "All we can do is wait, I suppose."

We stood there together. After a moment, Tophat came over to us. His manner had changed and he was looking almost respectful. I wondered if he now believed we really were the police because of our manner. Had he expected us, two young girls, to behave as his wife and her friend were behaving? Collapsing and weeping? Probably he had, I thought. He wasn't to know it wasn't the first time Verity and I had encountered violent death.

"Um... Miss? Officer?" Tophat was hovering a few feet away. Verity looked at me with a startled look and I frowned at her, hoping she wouldn't give me away.

"Yes, sir?"

"What – what will happen now?"

I cleared my throat, still keeping the same firm tone as I'd used before. "The other officers will be here very shortly, sir. I would imagine they would take statements from you, but you'll be able to leave after that."

Tophat nodded fervently, as if I'd just told him something incredibly profound. I smiled at him and then drew Verity away from him. Despite my outwardly calm demeanour, I was beginning to have a nasty little feeling of self-doubt. The chances were, as soon as the *real* police arrived, I'd be exposed as a fraud. My heart began to thump. Why had I done such a stupid and reckless thing? Another thought occurred to me which did nothing to calm my fears. Wasn't it actually a criminal offence to impersonate an officer of the law?

Oh God, oh God. I could feel cold sweat breaking out all over me. Why had I been so recklessly impulsive? Who on Earth did I think I was? I must have been mad.

"What's wrong?" Verity whispered. She must have noticed my increasingly green and clammy look. Then she snorted. "Apart from there being a dead body ten feet away from us?"

I dragged her even further away from Tophat and his group and told her what I'd said. She looked at me as though I'd just sprouted another head. "Are you quite mad, Joanie? What did you go and say a silly thing like that for?"

I groaned. "I don't *know*. I just wanted to make sure they didn't disturb the scene any more than they already had." Verity rolled her eyes. "Oh God, what am I going to do?"

Verity bit her lip. "Listen, if there's a problem, we'll just say he misheard you. I mean, it's not your fault that he mistook your meaning, is it?" She looked right into my eyes. "That's awfully dramatic behaviour from you, Joanie. Are you sure you don't actually have a secret longing to tread the boards yourself?"

Despite my panic, I couldn't help but smile. Verity could always make me laugh. "I blame *you*. You're a bad influence."

"Well, perhaps." The sound of heavy boots on the stairs preceded what seemed like a veritable flood of policemen pouring into the Gods. Verity squeezed my arm. "Hold hard, Joan. It's showtime."

AT FIRST IT SEEMED LIKE a ridiculous scrimmage, as the police surrounded the body. Verity and I drew back towards Tophat and his little group. Someone who I assumed was David the theatre manager, was standing by the doorway, talking to someone in plainclothes who looked quite senior. David was pulling at his hair and waving his arms about, and he looked in imminent danger of having some kind of fit. The senior-looking man was holding his hands out towards him, making soothing motions.

A uniformed officer detached himself from the crowd around the body and came over towards Verity and me. I could see another one making their way towards Tophat and tried to edge away a little so there would be more distance between us.

"Now, young ladies. Can you tell me what's been going on here?" The police officer was very tall and thin, with a bony jaw and an Adam's apple that bobbed up and down as he spoke. Verity and I exchanged glances.

"Would it be possible to talk somewhere a little quieter?" I asked. I *had* to get out of the room before Tophat pointed me out as 'another officer'.

Verity put a fluttering hand to her throat. "We've been trapped here with that – that *corpse* for what seems like hours, officer." She sounded weak and feeble, as if she was on the verge of collapse.

The policeman looked flustered. "Of course, of course. Follow me and we'll try and find somewhere for you ladies to sit down."

"Oh, thank you, officer," Verity said breathily. Despite my anguish at being unmasked as a fraud, I had to bite the inside of my cheek to keep from giggling. Talk about *me* going on the stage – with Verity, theatre's loss was domestic service's gain.

The policeman ushered us out of the Gods and towards the stairs. We were just coming to the top step of the flight when both Verity and I simultaneously saw who was walking up the stairs towards us. He looked just as he had when I'd last seen him, over a year ago now, dressed in his customary black suit with his beard and moustache neatly trimmed.

Inspector Marks caught sight of us both a second later and actually stopped dead, causing a minor pile-up in the group of people behind him. He took no notice. I could tell he recognised us straight away.

Verity and I stood on the landing like spare parts, waiting for the inspector to reach our level, which he did in just a few steps.

"Well, well, well." Inspector Marks' gaze went from my face to Verity's. For some reason, I found myself blushing. "Miss Hart and Miss Hunter. What in Heaven's name are you two ladies doing here?"

The police officer who'd escorted us from the room was looking from us to the inspector as if watching a tennis match. Inspector Marks noted this and smiled at the man pleasantly. "Thank you, officer—"

He raised his eyebrows and the policeman stammered out, "Constable Watkins, sir."

"Constable Watkins, of course. Thank you for bringing these ladies this far, but I can take them from here."

"Yes, sir. Of course, sir." Constable Watkins almost bobbed a curtsey as he turned and scurried back into the Gods. I didn't dare look at Verity for laughing.

Inspector Marks waited until he was out of earshot and then turned back to us, the smile dying on his face. "Please tell me you girls aren't mixed up in this?"

"We were only watching a play," Verity said indignantly. "That's all. It wasn't our fault somebody got stabbed to death virtually in front of us."

Inspector Marks looked at both of us in turn. "Is that what happened?"

He turned to me, then and gave me the look I remembered well. It's hard to describe but it was as if he really *saw* me – as if he was the only person ever to really see me, as I was and without judgement or criticism, or finding me wanting. It had warmed me before and it warmed me now.

"Yes," I said. "That's what it looked like to me. I think someone sat behind him, in the row behind him, and stabbed him through the back of the chair."

Inspector Marks's eyebrows rose. "Indeed, Miss Hart. Well, I'll see for myself in a minute." He stood back a little. "I'll talk to you ladies later. No, indeed, tomorrow." He glanced at the gold watch he wore on one wrist. "It's getting late and I'll wager you girls have work to do." Verity and I exchanged a rueful glance. Inspector Marks went on. "I'll let that young constable take a brief statement from both of you and you can be on your way. But—" His voice became emphatic. "I will have to speak to you both again."

"Of course, sir," I said. "We understand."

The inspector smiled. "You always do, Miss Hart." He shook his head for a moment. "You're wasted in your job, you know. Both of you."

And with that startling statement, he inclined his head to us courteously and was gone.

Chapter Three

THE DRAMATIC EVENTS OF THE evening had completely driven the news about Lord Cartwright from my mind. I'd stuffed the newspaper into my handbag as I'd got to the theatre and hadn't thought anything more about it until late that night, when Verity and I had finally got home and were preparing for bed. Verity had undressed first and was already under the covers by the time I got back from the bathroom. It seemed foolish to bring up such a contentious subject so late at night, and she was already almost asleep, so I merely put the newspaper on the bedside table and got into bed myself. For all the excitement of the evening, sleep came quickly, as it tended to do. I worked too hard every day to find getting to sleep a problem.

The clang of the alarm woke me as it did every morning. I groaned and slapped a hand onto the vibrating metal clock. Rubbing my eyes, I reluctantly sat up to see Verity already awake and sitting up in bed with yesterday's newspaper spread over her knees.

"Oh," I said reluctantly, and she looked across at me with a stricken face. "I meant to tell you last night but, well, things happened. I was distracted."

Verity put the paper back down on her lap, her shoulders sagging. She looked down at the headline. "Dorothy's going to be distraught."

I said nothing. What could I say that would be a comfort? It was true. Verity was lady's maid to Dorothy Drew, someone who, on the face of it, had everything. Dorothy was young, beautiful, high-born and rich. She was also someone whose father had died young, whose mother and brother had been murdered, and now her stepfather had been found not guilty of the murder both Verity and I knew he had committed.

I sat down on the bed next to Verity and patted her shoulder. "I know it's hard. I suppose at least he wasn't family. Not blood, I mean." I meant Lord Cartwright but a second after I said it I wished I hadn't. There had been too much blood spilled already.

I caught sight of the accursed alarm clock. "Oh Lord, look at the time. Mrs Watling will be after me."

Verity tried to smile. "We'll talk later, Joanie. Have a good morning. I suppose the inspector will be contacting us, won't he?"

I paused in my frantic dressing. "Golly, I'm not sure. Should we telephone?"

Verity looked down at the newspaper on her lap. Then, with a sudden movement, she screwed it up into a messy ball and threw it hard across the room. "God! Are we never to be free of all this...this nonsense?"

I felt guilty then. Although Verity and I had been instrumental in tracking down the murderers of Dorothy's family, it had meant a very big upheaval in our lives. Dorothy had moved back down to London after the dust settled and had taken most of the staff of Merisham Lodge, Lord Cartwright's summer residence, with her. I had been glad at the time – glad to still have a job, glad to be working with the cook, Mrs Watling, who was an amiable woman and a good employer to work under. I was still glad. As jobs went, this one really wasn't too bad. Plenty of time off, good food and most of the staff had worked together for long enough that most little annoyances between us had been smoothed away. But the shadow of what had happened at Merisham Lodge still hung over us. I suppose it always would.

I squeezed Verity's arm in farewell. "What are you up to today?"

Verity rolled her eyes. "Calming Dorothy down, by the looks of it. Do you think the newspapers will call?"

I hadn't even thought of that aspect of it. "I suppose they might. Mr Fenwick will head them off, though." Mr Fenwick was the butler, a rather ponderous and elderly gentleman but a very good butler. I was slightly surprised that he'd agreed to join the staff in Dorothy's establishment, having been butler to Lord Cartwright for so long, but then I suppose the scandal of Lord Cartwright's arrest and subsequent imprisonment on remand had meant that working for Dorothy probably seemed like the best option for a servant nearing retirement.

Lord Cartwright. I spared him a thought as I hurried down the stairs, tucking my hair up under my cap and trying to slide the pins in to fix it in place. Quite difficult without a mirror. What would Lord C do now he was free? Surely he would not be able to rejoin polite society? No, I decided, as I hurried into the kitchen, if I were him, I'd head off abroad somewhere. Somewhere far away.

Late as I was, at least Mrs Watling hadn't yet appeared in the kitchen. I hurriedly filled the kettle and put it in the hob. We didn't have a kitchen maid here, just the tweeny who helped out when she was needed, in between doing the fires and the floors and all the horrible jobs that I was very thankful I didn't have to do anymore. Dorothy's establishment wasn't large. She lived alone (well, alone apart from all the servants) and it was only really when she was entertaining that there was a frantic rush. In fact, it was more work looking after the servants' needs than it was dealing with the demands of the lady of the house.

Of course, that would change if she got married. I knew from Verity that there were several suitors keen on making an honest woman of her, but also nobody that Dorothy liked enough to relinquish her spinster status. She was now an extremely wealthy woman, having inherited her mother's entire estate, but she wasn't happy. Although I didn't see as much of her as Verity did, when I did spend time with her, I could see the unhappiness almost seeping out of her like a grey fog. Dorothy had always had a kind of languid, world-weary deportment – it was the fashion amongst rich young women, I'd noticed – but after the events at Merisham Lodge, it was as if that cynicism, that fatigue with life, had developed into a kind of armour, a shiny beetle-like carapace that Dorothy hid behind. Not that I could blame her, poor woman. She'd gone through enough in her short life to weary anyone.

The kettle whistled away to itself on the hob. I wrapped my hand in a tea towel to take it off the stove and poured the boiling water into the waiting teapot.

"Good morning, Joan." Mrs Watling had arrived in the kitchen. She always greeted me pleasantly, such a nice change from a few employers I'd had before. "How was your theatre trip?" She accepted the cup of tea I held out to her with thanks. "I suppose you've seen the papers?"

She meant the news about Lord Cartwright? Or did she? Had the murder at the theatre made the front pages already or wasn't it of sufficient importance to get a headline? I made a mental note that at some point that day I would go out and buy myself a newspaper.

"Was it a good play?" Mrs Watling asked, nodding in approval as she saw the preparations for breakfast already underway.

I was silent for a moment. Where to begin? For a moment I quailed at having to give her the news that Verity and I were now involved in another criminal case. It wasn't very fair, was it? We'd been innocent bystanders, just there for the play.

Mrs Watling was looking at me expectantly.

"Oh, well – it was, er, well – it was quite dramatic." I began breaking eggs into a bowl, my hands not quite steady.

Mrs Watling laughed. "Well, you were at the theatre, Joan!" Then she sighed and said "I could have done with a trip out last night too. Get away from the news. Miss Drew was in an awful state. Mrs Anstells said it took hours to calm her down. We could have done with Verity here."

"I can imagine. It was a shock." I was fed up with talking and thinking about Lord Cartwright but I could understand Mrs Watling wanting to hash it over. "I wonder what will happen now?"

"I imagine he'll go abroad," said Mrs Watling, echoing my thoughts of the morning. "There's nothing left for him here."

I seasoned the eggs and began whisking them. For a moment, I thought about the other murderers of Merisham Lodge, the ones who had been caught. They were both dead now, one hanged and one dying in prison whilst awaiting trial. The newspapers said it had been pneumonia but I wondered. Suicide seemed as likely to me.

I shook myself, trying to shake off the melancholy mood that was overwhelming me. To cap it all, I now had to tell Mrs Watling that I was expecting a visit from the police at any moment. Damn it to hell, I thought to myself viciously and gave the eggs an extra good beating as a way of working out my frustration.

VERITY CAME DOWN FROM THE upper floors of the house to collect Dorothy's breakfast tray. She caught my eye and inclined her head towards Mrs Watling, who at that moment was just leaving the room to talk to the delivery boy from the grocer who'd brought the day's supplies.

"Have you told her yet?" Verity hissed.

"I haven't had a chance," I said. "It was as much as I could do to get her off the subject of Lord C." I paused and then asked, "How is Dorothy?"

Verity pulled a face. "Not wonderful." She looked at the tray piled high with food and said "I don't think she'll be eating much of that. Sorry, Joanie."

I shrugged. It was out of my control so it didn't worry me too much.

"Talk to you later," Verity said, picking up the tray. She tipped me a wink and I grinned, rather reluctantly.

Mrs Watling bustled back with the grocery lists for tomorrow, while behind her the boy brought in the boxes and bags of food. I waited until he had left and then cleared my throat. "Um, Mrs Watling?"

"Yes, Joan?" She was only half listening to me, occupied as she was with checking off the list against the deliveries.

"Um, something rather strange happened at the theatre last night—" I began. Mrs Watling looked up at me, her attention caught and then, right on cue, the kitchen door opened to admit, first Mr Fenwick and then behind him, Detective Inspector Marks.

For a moment, I thought Mrs Watling was going to faint. I could see she recognised him straight away. It must have taken her right back to those awful days after the murder at Merisham Lodge.

"Detective Inspector Marks," she said, faintly.

"Mrs Watling, isn't it? Do excuse me for intruding. I assume Joan has let you know why I'm here?"

All three of them looked at me. I tried to smile

and explain but I didn't get much further than stammering out something about "I was just trying to say..."

"Ah, well, it's probably easiest if I just speak to Joan directly and she can put you in the picture, afterwards? Hmm?"

Mrs Watling nodded, her hand to her throat. Mr Fenwick stood, ponderously observing the scene. "Inspector, you may use my pantry if you would so wish," he said, after a moment.

I followed the inspector towards Mr Fenwick's room. Did Mrs Watling think that the inspector was here because of something to do with Lord Cartwright? Why hadn't I just taken the bull by the horns and told her it was because Verity and I were now mixed up in another murder?

Inwardly chastising myself, I sat down opposite Inspector Marks, folded my hands in my lap, and waited.

"Now, Miss Hart. Joan, if I may?" I nodded and the inspector went on. "What happened when you got to the theatre last night? Take your time and try and tell me everything."

I did take my time. I talked slowly and carefully, giving him time to write it in his notebook (I was a little amused to see he was still using the cheapest sort). I told him how I was late meeting Verity, how we'd had to find our seats in the dark. I told him that the Gods were relatively empty, just Verity and

I and Tophat's little group in front of us. I even shut my eyes, thinking back on the memory, trying to remember every last detail. Then I remembered the woman.

My eyes shot open. Inspector Marks must have seen the expression on my face because he leant forward a little.

"There was another woman there," I said. I could even picture her, that little glimpse that I'd had, just of the curve of her cloche hat and the momentary gleam of what little light there was from the jewellery around her neck. "She came in even later than we did. And I think—" I swallowed, suddenly realising something. "Yes, she did. She sat at the end of the row, *our* row, so directly behind the – the man who was killed."

"Give me as much of a description as you can," said Inspector Marks, writing busily. I did as best I could but I really had so little to go on.

"I barely saw her," I said honestly. I could hear the frustration in my voice. Why hadn't I looked more closely? "She had a cloche hat on and some sort of necklace or jewellery around her neck. She was fairly tall..." My voice trailed away. What I had to say sounded laughably weak.

"You can't tell me anything else? Was she old? Young?" I shook my head. "Pretty? Ugly?" I shook my head again, feeling helpless.

"I'm really sorry, sir," I said. "I just caught the briefest glimpse and then the curtain went up and the play began, and I didn't notice anything else. I really am sorry."

"Don't worry yourself, Miss Hart. Joan." The inspector spoke absently. He had that look on his face that I remembered from Merisham Lodge – the inward, preoccupied look of someone who had just had a flash of insight. I wondered what it was and whether he would share it.

There was a short silence. I gathered my courage together and asked, "Has the victim been identified yet, Inspector?"

Inspector Marks blinked and came back to himself. He half smiled. "I'm afraid not. Not yet." He hesitated and then added, "There was nothing on the body to identify it. No wallet, no letters, no papers."

I frowned. "That's unusual, isn't it, sir?"

"Yes it is," agreed the Inspector.

I talked almost to myself. "It's as if someone doesn't want him identified. Now why would that be?" I suddenly realised I was thinking out loud and almost blushed. It wasn't my place to speculate.

The Inspector was looking at me in a way I couldn't quite place. He leant forward again. "Now, another strange thing is that one of the other witnesses, a Mister George Parkinson, was under the impression that you were – how shall I put it? Working for the Metropolitan Police Force?"

Now I really did blush, a roaring tide of blood

that heated my cheeks and thumped in my ears. I looked down, twisting my hands in my lap. "I'm sorry, sir, I'm not sure why he got that impression. I think he may have misheard me." Inspector Marks arched an eyebrow and in the silence that followed, I rushed on with something a little more honest. "Sir, I'm so sorry but I didn't know what else to do. I could tell that unless I could get him to move back he would have been all over the body and destroying evidence and I – I just couldn't think of how – how to stop him—"

I was becoming incoherent – and tearful. I managed to shut myself up and stared down at my hands, blinking hard.

"I understand," Inspector Marks eventually said, and something loosened a little inside me. I almost gasped with relief. "But don't let there be any similar...misunderstandings again, Joan. Do you understand me?"

"Yes," I gasped. "I'm sorry—"

He raised a hand. "Let's leave it there for now, Joan. Is there anything else you can tell me?" I thought furiously, wanting there to be something so I could get back into his good books again, but there was nothing. I shook my head miserably.

"Well, here's my card if anything else occurs to you," he said. The look he gave me then was kind but dismissive. "I'll go and see Miss Hunter now, if she's available."

He got up and I scrambled to my feet, bobbing a curtsey. To my surprise, Inspector Marks reached out and shook my hand. "Thank you, Joan. We'll speak again soon." I was too surprised to say anything and just nodded dumbly.

He was on the verge of leaving the room when I said, on impulse, "I'm very sorry, sir, about the case – about the case with Lord Cartwright. It doesn't seem fair."

Inspector Marks stopped with his hand on the doorhandle. His shoulders seemed to slump a little before he turned back to face me. His face was rueful. "Oh, well, Joan. You win some, you lose some."

"Yes, I suppose you do, sir."

We regarded each other for a moment. Then he inclined his head, said goodbye, and left the room.

Chapter Four

I DIDN'T SEE VERITY FOR THE rest of the day, and I was kept busy, both with cooking and with answering Mrs Watling's frantic questions. By the end of the day, I was glad to crawl upstairs and into bed. I was just pulling the covers up to my neck when Verity came in.

"God, what a day." She slumped down on her bed, rubbing her temples. "The police and Dorothy. What a combination."

I forced my eyes open. "What did you tell them?"

Verity got up and began to undress, yawning hugely. When she'd managed to get her jaw under control and her dress off, she said "I just told them what happened. We got there just before curtain up, there weren't many people up there, I didn't notice anything untoward."

Verity's yawning was contagious. I covered my mouth and asked "Did you tell them about the woman?"

"What woman?"

"She came in after us, right before the stage lights came on. She sat at the end of the row, behind – behind the man that was killed."

Verity sat down on the edge of her bed and stared at me. "If that's right, Joanie, then surely she's the murderer."

I rubbed my eyes. I wished we could get to talk about these things when I wasn't already half asleep, but we were kept so busy that it didn't seem very likely to happen any time soon. "I suppose so."

"What did she look like?"

I yawned again. "I don't know. I told Inspector Marks that. I didn't see her face, she had a cloche hat and some sort of jewellery on, and that's all I can remember."

"How annoying." Verity gathered together her wash bag in preparation for her trip to the bathroom. It was a much nicer bathroom here than the one we'd had to use at Merisham Lodge, with new tiling and a fire, and fresh towels every couple of days. "Still, I suppose the police have got it under control."

"I don't know about that," I said, snuggling back down under the covers. "They haven't even identified the body yet."

"Oh, well..." Verity let the sentence trail off. Then she looked over at me with compassion. "Get some sleep, Joanie. You look all in."

"I will. Good night."

"Good night. I'll be quiet when I come back in."

"Thanks," I said, mumbling now, because I could feel unconsciousness gaining on me. I pulled the covers up to my neck and was almost immediately asleep.

THE NEXT DAY WAS A sunny one, which always affected my mood for the better. Although the kitchen was situated in the basement of the house, as was usual, I got up and wiped over the windows with some newspaper and vinegar, to let the maximum amount of sunlight in. Dorothy was dining out later, which meant there wasn't a huge meal to prepare. I had hopes that I might actually get a little bit of time to myself that afternoon.

Mrs Watling and I worked in uncharacteristic silence. I was thinking back on the night of the murder, running that moment when I'd noticed the woman arriving late back over in my mind. The more I re-ran it through my mind, the fuzzier it seemed to become. I was left wondering whether I'd actually imagined her, although I knew really that I hadn't.

Verity came back downstairs with Dorothy's breakfast tray, filled with empty dishes and –I noticed with a jump of excitement – the morning's newspaper. Verity said nothing but inclined her head very slightly towards it. I nodded, just as subtly. How was I going to get a moment to read it? I didn't think I could bear to wait until after lunch, when it seemed likely I might have a few hours to myself. Verity tipped me a wink and left the room.

"Is that the paper?" Mrs Watling asked, breaking her long silence. "What does it say? Is there anything in it about the murder?"

I gave her a glance of pure gratitude and grabbed it up. We sat down together at the kitchen table with the paper spread out before us and greedily absorbed the news.

"They still don't know who he is," I exclaimed, reading and musing aloud as I skimmed the paragraph. "Hmm... 'Police believe he might be foreign-born'. I wonder how they know that? His clothing, perhaps? 'The murder weapon hasn't yet been located'." I glanced up at Mrs Watling. "It doesn't sound as though they're much further forward."

Mrs Watling shook her head. "That might not be such a bad thing."

"How do you mean?"

Mrs Watling pushed her chair back from the table, as if the paper itself was contaminated. "If they can't find out who he was, then perhaps they won't find out who did it. And then it won't come to trial and you poor girls won't have to go through that whole rigmarole again."

I felt a jab of guilt. Both Verity and I had had to give evidence at the trial of the Merisham Lodge murderers. It had taken up a great deal of time, never a commodity we were rich in, and the scandal and newspaper interest had been huge. No sooner had that died down than the trial of Lord Cartwright had begun and the whole ridiculous circus started up again. I couldn't blame Mrs Watling for her apprehension that we'd all be dragged through that again.

"I don't think we have to worry about actually giving evidence or anything like that." I hastened to reassure her. "We were just witnesses after all, and not even really that. We were just there when it happened. It's not as if we actually *saw* anything." *Unfortunately*, I added to myself in the privacy of my own head.

"Well, I hope you're right, Joan. I do hope you're right."

I folded the newspaper up again and put it to one side on the dresser, for a later, more leisurely perusal. I returned to the bread I'd been in the middle of making, dusting my hands with flour and beginning to lift and slam the dough. It was satisfying work, if a little hard on the wrists. So the police thought the murder victim was foreign? Something occurred to me that hadn't before. Was this a gangster killing? Had the victim been part of a foreign criminal gang? There had been some trouble recently in the West End, fights and stabbings between rival criminal gangs. Was this murder connected with those incidents?

There was a knock on the kitchen door that almost made me jump, bringing me back to reality as it did. Mrs Watling opened it to see one of the local urchins standing there, hopping from foot to foot and waving an envelope in one dirty mitt.

"Got a message for Miss Verity 'Unter," he said, importantly.

"I'll give it to her," said Mrs Watling, plucking it from the child's grubby fingers.

"I was tol' you'd give me a penny for giving it to 'er."

"Oh, you were, were you?" Mrs Watling looked down at the eager little figure with a half smile. "Wait here." She went over to the dresser and retrieved a penny from her purse and a biscuit, fresh baked that morning, from the biscuit tin. "Go on, here you go. Be off with you."

I smiled. Mrs Watling could be sharp sometimes but she was kind. Given some of the employers I'd had before, that meant a lot to me. "Shall I take that up to Verity?" I knew she'd say yes – Mrs Watling's legs were too old and tired to want to climb any more stairs than she had to.

"Yes, Joan. You'd better take it up now, it might be something to do with Her Ladyship."

Gladly, I snatched off my apron, washed the flour and dough from my hands, and made for the stairs. There were five flights in this house but at least we all got to use the one main staircase – there wasn't the servants staircase that I'd hated so much in the other houses I'd worked in. Despite the steep climb, it was a pleasant journey, given that I could take in all the lovely ornaments dotted about, the flowers and paintings all arranged with Dorothy's exquisite taste. Of course, she had the money to indulge it.

I found Verity in Dorothy's bathroom, cleaning and tidying it. The air was steamy and sweet-scented – Dorothy had obviously not long finished her bath.

"Hello, Joanie. What have you got there?"

I handed over the note. Verity raised her eyebrows and opened it.

"It's from Tommy," she said after scanning it. "He wants to know if we're free for tea this afternoon."

"Does he? Why's that?"

Verity gave me a wry look. "Wants to chew over the gossip from the murder, I would think. You know what actors are like."

"He wants to meet today?" By a small miracle, I realised that I might actually be free. I told Verity as much. "What about you, V? Will Dorothy let you go?"

Verity chewed her lip. "Actually, you know, I think she might. I'm out with her all evening so she might let me have a few hours to myself. Besides—"

She looked mischevious. "If there's gossip to be had, Dorothy is going to want to know about it."

I clapped my hands together with glee, as happy with the prospect of finding out more about what had happened at the theatre that night as with the thought of a few hours of relative freedom.

"I'll telephone Tommy," Verity said, bending once again to rub the water droplets from the bath with a small towel. "I'll say we'll meet him in the pub by the theatre at three o'clock. That suit you, Joanie?"

"Perfect." I gave her a cheery wave and said goodbye. I almost bounded down the stairs, so happy was I at the thought of what the afternoon had to bring.

AT ABOUT TWO AND TWENTY past the hour, Verity came into the kitchen smartly dressed in her blue velvet cloche and grey velvet coat. I reached for my own brown coat, trying to repress a pang of envy. Verity's clothes were mostly discards of Dorothy's but they were originally very expensive and beautifully cut, and Verity always looked wonderfully smart. I tried to arrange my hair a little more attractively, looking into the small looking glass that hung over by the back door. I knew a kitchen maid was never going to look as chic and attractive as a lady's maid but, I thought wistfully, it would be nice if for once

I could feel like the pretty one, rather than the plain homely friend.

I made an effort and shook off my melancholy thoughts. Verity was my best friend – it wasn't her fault she was prettier than me. I thought of all the generous gifts she'd given me, sharing out the spoils from Dorothy, and felt bad for feeling envious.

"Ready, Joan?" she asked, giving me a big grin in the mirror while she stood behind me. I smiled back, glad that my uncharitable thoughts hadn't shown on my face.

I pinched some colour into my cheeks, touched up my lipstick and straightened my hat. "I'm ready."

Mrs Watling came through from her parlour to say goodbye. "Have a lovely afternoon, girls. Joan, make sure you're back at six o'clock so we can start dishing up the dinner."

I repressed a sigh. It wasn't Mrs Watling's fault but I hated being reminded of the work to come when I was about to have an afternoon off.

We said goodbye and walked sedately out of the kitchen door. As soon as we were out of sight, we tore up the basement steps like a pair of puppies, giggling with exhilaration at the few hours of freedom we'd have to enjoy.

Chapter Five

Tommy Vance was Verity's mother's brother; a much younger brother, which meant that he was now only in his late twenties. He'd been an actor for his whole adult life, having virtually been born into the theatre. Like Verity, he had a lovely singing voice and had performed in music hall, as well as repertory theatre, and now the West End. He was nice too, fun and cheerful and, while not exactly handsome, he had the same vivacity that Verity possessed. I knew very well he'd never be romantically interested in me so I had to give myself quite a stern talking to every time we met, to make sure that I wouldn't fall in love with him.

We all met that afternoon at the White Horse, a public house right by the Connault Theatre. I suppose if I'd thought about it, I would have thought the theatre would have been closed and the show's run brought to a halt. Apparently, that wasn't the case.

"Not a bit of it," Tommy cried as he brought our

drinks to the table. "Why, we're sold out for the next two weeks! Nothing like a bloodthirsty murder to bring in the bums on seats."

I bit back a giggle. "Really? People are still coming to see the show?"

"Absolutely, Joan. Why, I think we're even talking about extending the run." He looked contrite for a moment. "Of course, it's terrible with what happened but if people do want to see the show, it seems silly not to indulge them."

Verity was grinning. "I've solved the murder, Joan." I looked at her, startled. She went on, beginning to laugh. "It was David, the theatre manager. He did it to get the audience in."

I shot her a reproving look but it was tempered by the fact that I couldn't help but laugh too. "Come on, V."

Verity sobered up. "I know. It's not really funny."

Tommy leant forward. "So, I heard you girls were actually *there*. Sitting next to the murderer!"

"Not quite." Verity threw the rest of her drink down her throat like a sailor. "But not far off. We were sitting about two seats away."

"Lord." Tommy gave a theatrical shiver. "I hear the police don't even know who the victim *is*. You girls didn't recognise him, or anything like that?"

I shook my head. "I'd never seen him before in my life." I thought of what I'd read in the newspaper that morning. "They seemed to think he was foreign. I don't know how they know that, though."

"Here, Tommy, get us another drink, please," said Verity, shoving a ten bob note over the table towards him. "We've got to get back in an hour, may as well make the most of it." I shook my head as Tommy raised his eyebrows in a questioning sort of way towards me. I wasn't used to alcohol and didn't want to have to go back to work tipsy. Verity was much more sophisticated than me in that department – well, being lady's maid to Dorothy meant she often shared a bottle of wine over dinner with her employer, not to mention accompanying her out for cocktails occasionally.

When Tommy returned, Verity leant forward. "Now we've told you *our* side of what happened, why don't you tell us what happened backstage after the police shut down the show?"

Tommy raised his hands in the air. "Verity, my dear, I'm sure you can imagine it. Utter chaos! Costume girls screaming, the orchestra milling around like Piccadilly Circus and as for Caroline—"

"Yes?" I said, leaning forward, eager to find out how the star of the show had reacted.

Tommy rolled his eyes skyward. "Well, she left no emotion unturned, shall we say." He looked up and a flicker of surprise went across his face. "Well, well, talk of the devil. You'll be able to ask her yourself."

Startled, I looked up and saw Caroline Carpenter herself approaching our table. A man accompanied her who, after a moment, I recognised as Aldous Smith. Scarcely able to believe it, I must have looked a sight with my mouth agape – before a sharp blow from Verity's elbow brought me back to my senses.

"Tommy, darling, I wondered where you'd got to." Caroline was a vision in fur wraps, a cunning little hat pulled down over one eye. "David's having hysterics – something about the police visiting." That made me sit up a little. By now, Tommy had risen to his feet and ushered Caroline into a spare chair, next to Verity. She bestowed a kind, somewhat condescending smile upon Verity and me.

"Of course, I know your niece very slightly," she said, once Tommy had made the introductions. "And Miss Hart, how nice to meet you." She waved a hand backwards at Aldous Smith who was hovering behind her shoulder. "Meet my other leading man, Aldous Smith. Aldous, stop fluttering about behind me and find yourself a seat."

I watched Aldous move smartly over to where there was a spare chair and bring it back to the table. He was very handsome close-up, even more so than he'd been on the stage, with fine cheekbones and a pair of rosebud lips that I would have killed for. For all his looks, he seemed somewhat shy and awkward, and he subsided onto his seat, saying nothing. A second later, he jumped up again to take

Caroline's marvellous fur coat and took it over to where there were some coat hooks on the wall.

Caroline pulled out a tortoiseshell cigarette case, offered them around and then accepted Tommy's light. I watched Aldous surreptiously return his lighter to his jacket pocket and bit down on a giggle. What must it be like to be Caroline? To have men dancing attendance on you, to swan around in your furs, having your cigarettes lit for you? Not that anyone would ever light my cigarettes for me, as I didn't smoke. I tried to occasionally, because anyone who was anyone smoked and I didn't want to be thought unsophisticated, but I just didn't like it. I couldn't stand the hot, choky feeling in my mouth and really, how sophisticated would I actually look if I stood there, turning green and spluttering half to death?

"So, darling," Tommy was saying to Caroline. "The police have been talking to you? What on Earth did they want?"

"Oh, no, darling, they haven't yet talked to me. I don't know why not," she added, looking a little chagrined. "No, they just wanted to see David about something or other. Access to the theatre, something like that."

"They will be talking to us all," Aldous Smith said abruptly. It was the first time he'd spoken and his voice was unexpectedly deep. "They'll want to talk to us all, to see if we know anything about it."

Caroline Carpenter gave him a glance that seemed a little annoyed. "Well, I can't see what good that can do. For heaven's sake, we were on stage for half the night, blinded by the lights. The chances of us having seen anything at all are frankly remote."

Aldous said nothing in return. He simply frowned and stared down at the table.

I wondered whether Verity and I should tell Caroline that we'd actually been there, in the part of the theatre in which the murder had taken place. I decided against it, though. It sounded – well, as if I were showing off a bit. And the presence of this fine actress and her companion had me both star-struck and tongue-tied.

Caroline had pulled off her fine leather gloves to pick up her drink and I noticed the large diamond cluster on the ring finger of her left hand. She must be engaged to be married. For all that I love the theatre, I don't really read the gossip columns so I had no idea who her fiancé was. I resolved to ask Verity on the way home – she was sure to know.

Caroline and Tommy were deep in a technical-sounding discussion about voice projection. Verity was attempting to talk to Aldous Smith but not getting very far – he was answering her, but mostly in monosyllables. I wondered whether what he'd said about the police was true. Would they question all of the actors, the stage-hands and the musicians? I decided he was probably right – Inspector Marks was nothing but thorough.

It was then I realised the time and sat up with an exclamation that made everyone stop talking and look at me. I felt my cheeks grow hot. "Sorry, everyone but I've just realised I need to get back—" I stopped myself saying *to work*. I didn't want the actors to know I was a servant. Ridiculous really – Tommy knew already and he was such a gossip that it was probably common knowledge around the theatre that Tommy's niece and her friend worked in service.

Verity, bless her, didn't argue. She quipped something about there being 'no rest for the wicked', which made Caroline smile, and we stood up and fetched our coats. I surreptiously stroked Caroline's fur, which was hanging next to my shabby old jacket – it felt wonderful. It was hard to resist the urge to bury my face in it.

"So long, my darlings." Tommy gave us both a smacking kiss on the cheek. "Come back and see the play again sometime. You might even get to watch the second act."

"We will." Verity gave him a hug. "Keep us posted on any developments, Tommy. You know what I mean?"

He winked at her. "I certainly do."

Caroline Carpenter gave us a dazzling, dismissive smile and a wave of her hand. The diamond on her ring finger flashed like a little star under the dim overhead light. Aldous Smith grunted something that could have been a goodbye.

"I CAN'T BELIEVE WE GOT to meet Caroline Carpenter," I enthused on the way home. "And Aldous Smith as well." I paused. "He's a bit strange, isn't he?"

"He's just a bit shy," Verity said. "I've met him before, and he's been quite different."

"Well, Caroline is as charming as I thought she'd be."

"Mmm." Verity adjusted her hat. "God, Joanie, did you see the size of that engagement ring?"

"How could I miss it?" I said with feeling. "Who's she engaged to, anyway?"

"Sir Nicholas Holmes."

I paused. "Now, from the way you just said that, it sounds like he's someone quite impressive, but I have absolutely no idea who he is."

Verity grinned. "He's an MP. I don't know where his constituency is, or anything like that, though."

"An MP and an actress?" I considered this for a moment.

"Oh, come on, Joanie, acting is quite respectable now. Especially if you're good at it and get plenty of good press, like Caroline does."

"I suppose so." We'd reached the entrance to the underground station by now and began walking down the steps, into the fug of dirt-laden steam and the smell of oil. We joined the back of the queue waiting for the guard to open the metal gates to allow access to the train.

It was too crowded and noisy to talk in the third class carriage. I stood, hanging onto the leather strap that dangled from the ceiling and tried to keep my balance in the rocking, swaying, clattering train. I thought about many things: Caroline Carpenter's talent and beauty, Tommy's lovely manners, what it must be like to work in a theatre. As we began to draw near our stop, the hard work lying ahead of me that night began to intrude and I sighed a little and mentally began to plan out all the things I had to do that night, thoughts of the murder and of the theatre forgotten.

Chapter Six

WHEN I WOKE UP THE next morning, Verity was already awake, sitting up in her bed with a shawl around her shoulders as she read a letter. I sat up myself, shivering. Nancy, one of the two housemaids, hadn't yet been in to light our fire and the room was freezing.

"Morning," Verity said absently, without looking up from her letter.

"Morning," I said, yawning. "Sorry. Who's the letter from?"

"Nora."

Now I did sit up properly. Nora had been a friend of Verity's and mine, a parlourmaid at Merisham Lodge. She'd got herself in trouble – no, that was a stupid way of putting it – she'd *found* herself in trouble, and both Verity and I had tried to help her. From what Verity had told me, a sympathetic Dorothy had arranged for a procedure to help Nora get rid of the baby. (I didn't know exactly what this was and Verity refused to tell me). Sadly, despite the immediate problem being solved, neither the combined charm of Verity and Dorothy could persuade Mrs Anstells to keep Nora on in her position. I hadn't witnessed the discussion that took place between the lady of the house and the head housekeeper, but Verity had and relayed the gist of it to me later. "No, madam could surely not countenance Nora remaining in her post, no indeed. To keep her on would be to approve of the depravity of the girl's wanton behaviour and would set a terrible example to the other young maids in the house. No, indeed, her ladyship would surely not countenance such a thing and if that indeed was the case, then she, Mrs Anstells herself, would no longer be able to remain in the employ of such a household...", Verity had said, rolling her eyes. The fact remained that Dorothy had to dismiss Nora or risk losing her housekeeper, so away poor Nora had to go. The only consolation was that Dorothy promised to write her a decent reference.

"I didn't know she'd written to you," I exclaimed, going over to Verity's bed and getting in beside her. It was a squeeze and she flinched away from my cold feet.

"Ow, Joan, your feet are freezing. Here, I'll get up and you read Nora's letter." She threw back the bedclothes to get out and threw them back over me. "Where's bloody Nancy with the coals?" Just as she said that, there was a tap at the door and

51

Nancy hurried in, looking flushed and bearing the welcome sight of the brass coal scuttle in one hand.

"About bloody time," Verity grumbled, but she helped Nancy rake out the ashes and set the fire. Soon a merry blaze was warming the room and Nancy hurried out again.

I read through Nora's letter, feeling a mixture of relief and despair. Nora had had to go home after she was dismissed and, from the sounds of it, had had to take whatever job she could get; that of a maid of all work at a solicitor's house near her home village. I suppose it was a job *but*... I looked around at Verity and my room, which for a servant's room was really quite comfortable. We had an electric bedside light, a wardrobe each – well, to be fair, part of Verity's job was to dress well and advise her mistress on fashion, so she needed more clothes storage space than I did – and underfoot was a rug rather than cold, bare floorboards.

I caught sight of the time. "Oh, help. I'm late!" I jumped out of bed and began to dress hurriedly, washing myself quickly in the washbowl that stood on the dresser and shrieking at the touch of the icy water.

"See you later," I said to Verity, but she called me back just as I was about to hurry out of the door.

"Oh, Joan, Dorothy might have already mentioned this to Mrs Watling but she's having a guest to dinner tonight."

"Very well." I waited for her to go on. She didn't normally give me this kind of warning.

"Don't you want to know who it is?"

I looked at her expressively. "Who is it?"

Verity smiled. "Inspector Marks."

I looked at her again. "Inspector Marks is dining here tonight?"

Verity nodded. "Yes, she made me call him up the other night and invite him to dinner. Out of the blue. I suppose she wants to chew over what happened with the collapse of Lord C's case."

I still had my hand on the door handle but I made no move to leave. "Perhaps," I said slowly. "She wouldn't – it wouldn't be because of this new case, would it?" I answered my own question. "No, how could it? What would Dorothy have to do with that?"

Verity was getting dressed herself by now. "Well, I just thought I'd better let you know."

"Oh, help." Something else had occurred to me. "It's Mrs Watling's evening out tonight. I suppose I'll be doing the whole meal."

"You'll be fine," Verity said in a cheerful voice, slightly muffled by the blouse she was pulling over her head. "Do that clear soup thing, he'll love that."

"That's a *starter*."

"So, start with that." Her red head emerged from the blouse, grinning at me. I rolled my eyes, flapped a hand in goodbye, and left the room.

MRS WATLING HADN'T YET APPEARED when I rushed into the kitchen, thankfully, although Doris, the tweeny, had already got the range alight and the kettle boiling. I gave her a warm smile of approval as I tied on my apron.

As we prepared the breakfasts, I let myself think about the strangeness of Dorothy inviting Inspector Marks to dine. He wasn't gentry. He wasn't fashionable society. Yes, he was very senior in his profession but that wouldn't normally be enough for Dorothy to go the trouble of putting on a three course meal for him. Surely it was just because she wanted to talk to him about the trial of Lord Cartwright and why it had failed? What other explanation could there be?

I prepared Dorothy's tray for Verity to take up and began setting the table in the servants' hall for breakfast. There were nine staff that lived in; Mr Fenwick, Mrs Anstells, Mrs Watling, myself and Verity; the two housemaids, Nancy and Margaret, who also acted as parlour maids when necessary; Andrew, the footman who doubled as the chauffeur, and little Doris, the between maid. Between us all, there was a lot of food to prepare, although nothing like the quantities that had been demanded at Merisham Lodge. As we sat down to breakfast, I was beginning to worry about the meal I would be expected to make for the dinner party that night. Would Dorothy choose the menu? It would be the first meal that I would have had to prepare completely on my own, although, thinking about it, I supposed I would have Doris to help me. I shovelled in bacon and eggs without really tasting anything, thinking of menus and presentation and whether I'd need to consult with Mr Fenwick on the wine. If it was up to me to chose the menu, then I'd do roast beef, I decided. Roast beef with all the trimmings, with the clear soup to start and a fancy pudding. Men liked meat, didn't they? Inspector Marks probably wasn't that used to fine dining, was he? So there was nothing to worry about, was there?

"Joan? Joan?"

I came to with a start, realising Mrs Watling was addressing me. "Sorry, what was that?"

"Stop woolgathering, my girl. Her ladyship wants to see you upstairs."

"Me?" I said ungrammatically in surprise.

"Yes, you. Come on, look lively. You know I'm out tonight, don't you?" I nodded. "Don't you worry," added Mrs Watling kindly, having noticed my look of panic. "There's nothing much to it, and it's not like you don't know how to cook. Let me know what her ladyship wants and we'll run through it together." I flashed her a grateful look as I set off for the stairs.

DOROTHY WAS IN THE MAIN drawing room, wearing

her cream satin house pyjamas, the little Turkish slippers that ended in droll little bells on the curly toes, her golden hair pin-curled and clipped to her head and covered in a filmy net of chiffon. As I waited respectfully just inside the door, I wondered if I'd ever seen Dorothy in less than a full face of make-up. I didn't think I had.

"Oh, Joan, hullo. Do come in and sit down at the table. I thought we'd run through the dishes for tonight – I suppose Verity has told you?"

"That you're expecting Inspector Marks to dinner? Yes, my lady, she has."

"Good, then you're forewarned," said Dorothy, approvingly. She sat down gracefully in one of the seats at the table and gestured to the other. I seated myself cautiously, feeling out of place in my uniform in this genteel, feminine room. I would have loved to have had a proper look around but there was little chance of that.

Dorothy was a relaxed and generous employer and a modern woman, but there was still no way on Earth that I was going to be able to ask her exactly why she'd asked the inspector to dinner. That would have been dreadfully impertinent. As she leant forward over the sheet of paper on which she'd scrawled suggestions for the menu, I could smell her distinctive perfume. I didn't know the name of it but it was French and very expensive, so Verity had said. Dorothy always smelt of it, mixed with a sophisticated undertone of cigarette smoke, but today there was a discordant note in her scent, something that made my nostrils flare. After a moment, I realised what it was. Brandy.

I looked around the room surreptitiously, but I couldn't see a glass or a bottle anywhere. On the table was a cooling tea pot and a cup and saucer with the brackish dregs of tea leaves in the bottom of it. I sniffed again, wondering if I was mistaken. After all, it was barely ten o'clock in the morning, far too early even for Dorothy to have had a cocktail. I must have been mistaken. Perhaps some had been spilled on the carpet in here or something.

I made an effort to bring my attention back to what Dorothy was saying. She sounded just as she normally did, with the same sort of rich, dark drawling voice as she always had.

"—and I thought a sort of seafood medley might be nice as an accompaniment to the lobster, don't you think?"

I stared blankly at the elegant scrawl of Dorothy's handwriting and swallowed. Did I dare say what I thought?

"Joan?" she prompted.

"I'm sorry, my lady, I didn't mean to be inattentive. It was just – I wondered whether this menu might be a little – a little, um, sophisticated for Inspector Marks. I mean, it's absolutely delicious, mouthwatering, my lady, it's just that I wonder whether he might – um, he might—" I trailed off, feeling myself beginning to blush. Why couldn't I just keep my big mouth shut? What did it matter, anyway? I just want to impress him, I thought to myself and then I did blush, a great wash of heat climbing into my face.

I thought Dorothy might be annoyed with me but she was lighting a cigarette with a smile on her face. "Do you think so, Joan? I wonder—" She regarded the menu she scribbled down, pursing her bright red lips and frowning. "Well, he is a *policeman* after all. You'd know more about that level of society than I would." I hoped she didn't notice the wince I gave at that but she wasn't looking at me. "No, no, perhaps you're right." She picked up her fountain pen and scored through her words with a flourish. "You're quite right. So, what do you suggest?"

AFTER MY SUGGESTION OF ROAST beef had been well received, we settled on the soup, the h'ordeuves and the dessert. I was dismissed with a kindly smile and with the tea tray in my hands. I carried it carefully back down the stairs, china chinking musically away.

"So what's it going to be?" asked Mrs Watling as I came back into the kitchen and thankfully put the tray down on the table.

"Roast beef, with French onion soup to start. A lemon tart to finish."

"Nice and plain," said Mrs Watling approvingly. "Not like her ladyship. Did you suggest that?" I nodded. "Well, good for you, Joan. You've got nothing to worry about tonight. Ring up the butcher now and get them to send you round the joint, you know what that delivery boy is like, he's never on time."

I nodded again, trying to hide my disquiet. I wasn't used to talking on the telephone and didn't much like doing it. Still, Mrs Watling was right – I didn't want to be hanging about later waiting for the main course to arrive.

The downstairs telephone was situated just outside Mr Fenwick's parlour. As I picked up the receiver and looked up the number of the butchers, on the list that was pinned up to the wall, I had a very unwelcome thought, one that seemed to come out of nowhere. Dorothy wasn't inviting Inspector Marks to dinner because – because she was *sweet* on him? Because she was romantically interested in him? Don't be stupid, I told myself fiercely, staring blindly at the list of telephone numbers. She wouldn't be interested in a *policeman* as a beau, even if he were a chief inspector. Not Dorothy, surely? I pushed the thought of her previous lover, Simon Snailer, from my mind. He'd been quite a disreputable artist-type, so it wasn't as though she wasn't used to slumming it... I felt very disloyal and uncomfortable even thinking those thoughts, both about Dorothy and about Inspector Marks. What business was it of mine, anyway?

I realised I knew nothing about Inspector Marks's home life. Perhaps he was married anyway. Did he have children? I didn't even really know how old he was, except he was quite young to be in such a senior position. Possibly, he wasn't even yet forty.

It's none of your business, Joan. Just cook a superb meal and let that be your reward. Stop getting ideas above your station. I told myself all that in a fierce inner whisper and then put my hand to the dial, determined not to think about it anymore.

Chapter Seven

I HEARD THE FRONT DOORBELL RING at precisely eight o'clock, and a few moments later, the ponderous tread of Mr Fenwick moved over the floorboards above my head as he went to answer it. The anxiety inside me screwed a notch tighter. The beef was done to a turn and resting in the warming part of the oven, the potatoes and carrots were crisping up nicely. Doris was mashing up the cooked swede with lots of butter.

"More salt and pepper," I said as I passed her with the roasting tin in my hands. Now I could appreciate how snappy Mrs Watling could get during the preparation for a big dinner party. This was just for two and it was hard enough getting everything cooked and presented to perfection. I caught the tail end of the sulky look Doris gave me but I was too busy making the gravy to really notice.

I transferred the soup to the big-bellied serving bowl, adding the layer of cheese and toasted bread slices to the top, and then slid it back into the oven for one last warm-through. The beef, vegetables, gravy and condiments were transferred to the trays that Andrew and Mr Fenwick would carry up to the dining room before serving the meal. I wasn't expected to wait at the table here, although I had on occasion at Merisham Lodge. It was a job I'd always hated, being afraid that I'd spill something or drop a plate with disastrous results, but perversely, I now wished I was able to go up and work in the dining room. I admitted to myself, with some shame, that I wanted to be there in the room to see what Dorothy and Inspector Marks were talking about.

I'd been so flurried, what with getting everything ready for their dinner, that I'd completely forgotten about preparing anything for the servants. Frantically, I looked around the kitchen as if a fully cooked meal would suddenly miraculously spring into existence.

Verity came through the door with a book in her hand. "What's wrong? You look as if you're about to drop."

"I forgot to get the servants' meal," I hissed. Near tears, I tore open the door of the refrigerator and glared into it. Oh, praise be to the Lord and Mrs Watling. I'd forgotten about the big pot of beef stew she'd made yesterday. Grabbing it with both hands, I ran with it to the range and shoved it inside to heat up. Some herb dumplings to accompany it wouldn't take much time at all.

"Panic over?" Verity asked, sitting down at the table and opening her book.

I nodded, rolling my eyes. While the stew was heating up, I got on with the dumplings, instructing Doris to peel some extra carrots and mash some more swede. When we all finally sat down, the table was gratifyingly covered in various dishes and there were appreciative comments, especially from the men. I remembered Mrs Watling telling me that, gentleman or working man, men liked meat. Perhaps that was why I'd been so insistent on the roast beef for Inspector Marks.

Verity sat next to me at the dinner table as was usual. "When do you next have a night off?" she asked.

I thought about it. "On Tuesday. Why?"

"Fancy going to the theatre again?"

I looked at her, feeling a thump of both excitement and anxiety. "The theatre? You mean, to see Tommy's play again?"

Verity nodded. "He promised me tickets. And, we can go backstage afterwards. You know. Talk to people."

The excitement was there and sharper now. I *wanted* to talk to people, to all the stage hands and the actors and the people who'd been there on the night of the murder. "That would be wonderful," I murmured, trying to keep my voice steady. "I'm sure it'll be fine but I'll check with Mrs Watling."

"Good." Verity took care of the last forkful

of stew on her plate and then daintily wiped her mouth with the rough napkins we used below stairs. She jerked her head up to the ceiling. "What do you think they're talking about, up there?"

I knew exactly who she meant. So Verity had been puzzling over it too? "I don't know," I said, reluctantly. And then, because I had to know, I leant a little closer and whispered, "Dorothy's not – not *interested* in the inspector, is she?"

Verity laughed. "I doubt it. Dorothy might like to *dabble* with men of a different class but she'd hardly go so low as a policeman. Come on, Joan."

I sat back, feeling unaccountably relieved. "Well, that's what I thought too, to be honest."

Verity pushed her chair back, shaking her head. "Want me to help you clear up? Haven't you got the pudding to do?"

I got up too, thankful that at least I had that under control. "All done and waiting to be taken up. If you could wipe the kitchen table down for me, that would be wonderful."

"Consider it done."

GRADUALLY THE SERVANTS' HALL EMPTIED of staff until there was only Doris, Verity and me left. I left Doris to get on with the washing up in the scullery and got Andrew to take the coffee and cheeseboard up to the dining room. *Almost over...* Wearily, I began hanging up the copper pans and putting the washed utensils away.

The dining room bell jangled, and both Verity and I looked up in surprise. "I'll go," she said, getting to her feet with a groan. Nodding, I waved a tired hand at her as she left the room.

I helped Doris with the last of the washing up and then sent her up to her room at the top of the house, which she shared with Nancy. I was expecting Mrs Watling back at any moment – it was past eleven o'clock. What were the chances of Dorothy and Inspector Marks wanting any more refreshments? I wavered for a moment and then re-filled the kettle, just in case they decided to go on chatting into the night.

There was a clearing of a masculine throat behind me that made me jump. I turned around to find Inspector Marks was standing in the doorway of the kitchen.

"Sorry to startle you, Miss Hart," he said cheer-fully, coming in. I was suddenly very conscious of my dirty apron and the strands of hair that had escaped from my cap and had plastered themselves to my forehead as I had stood, sweating, over the stove. "I just wanted to come down and thank you for a really excellent dinner."

I smiled. "It was my pleasure, sir. I'm glad you enjoyed it."

"I haven't enjoyed a meal like that in a long

time. The beef was done to perfection." I was feeling rather hot by now, under such praise. The inspector stood for a moment, looking about him. I don't suppose he got to go into many kitchens during his usual working day.

There was a slightly awkward silence then. I could hear the faint clangs of expanding metal as the kettle began to heat up on the gas.

"Can I bring you anything else, sir?" I asked.

The inspector looked at the kettle. "Well, if you're not too tired, I wouldn't say no to a cup of tea."

"Oh, certainly." I began to worry about where the good cups were. "Would her ladyship like a tray sent up?"

"No, I meant, I'd quite like to have a cup of tea with you. Down here. If that's not too much trouble?"

"Of course not," I said, a little too quickly. I covered over my confusion by busying myself with the kettle and the teapot.

The kettle seemed to take an absolute age to boil. I was being as busy as possible, putting cups out (I managed to find a few good ones at the back of the dresser) and warming the pot and hunting out some biscuits from the batch Mrs Watling had baked yesterday. Still, the silence between us stretched out uncomfortably, and in the end I broke it by asking a question he'd already answered. "So, the meal was to your liking, sir?"

He smiled. "It was wonderful, Joan. Perhaps I was a bit hasty when I told you you were wasted in your job."

I remembered him saying that, on the staircase at the theatre. All of a sudden, my nervousness fell away. He *wanted* to talk to me, and if I had read things rightly, he wanted to talk to me about the case at the theatre. I poured him a cup of tea, my hands quite steady now, proffered the milk and sugar and then sat down opposite him at the kitchen table. After a moment, I poured myself a cup, if only to have something for my hands to do.

"Well, Miss Hart." The inspector took a neat sip from his cup. "Here we are again."

I took a deep breath. "You can call me Joan, sir. If you'd like."

"Joan. Thank you." He inclined his head courteously. "Well, Joan, I suppose you've been wondering why I accepted Miss Drew's invitation tonight – well, perhaps not so much why I accepted it, more what we were talking about. Perhaps that's more what you were thinking?"

"Well, I was, to be honest," I said frankly. "I can only assume it had something to do with the Lord Cartwright case."

"You thought rightly. Miss Drew wanted to go over, in great detail, exactly where I'd gone wrong."

"Oh." I tried to read his tone but it was neutral.

Then the inspector smiled ruefully. "I must say,

she sugared the pill rather well with that delightful dinner. Normally when I get hauled over the coals it's standing on the cold linoleum of my superior's office floor."

I smiled, relieved. "Her ladyship would never want a guest to go without a good dinner, no matter why they were here."

"I agree. True breeding there." He looked as though he was going to say something else then but obviously thought better of it.

There was another silence that threatened awkwardness again. I decided to be bold. "Can I ask you if you're any further forward with the murder case at the theatre, sir?"

Inspector Marks leant back in his chair and sighed. "Well, as you'll no doubt see from the papers tomorrow, the body has finally been identified." I sat forward in excitement and he shook his head ruefully at me. "However, there's a strong suspicion that he was actually travelling under a false name and his real identity hasn't yet been uncovered."

"Was he a spy?" I asked, fascinated.

"Now, that's a good question, Joan. I'd like very much to know that." The inspector was silent for a moment and then added, "There was something so clinical about his death – almost like an execution. A professional murder, if you will."

I took a sip of my tea. His words had just made me recall something I'd thought of earlier, when

I was thinking about how Verity and I had sat in those theatre seats, our eyes glued to the action on stage.

"Sir, if I may…" I faltered and then took a deep breath. "I've been thinking about that, about how he was killed, I mean. And I think it's something to do with the theatre."

Inspector Marks looked at me. "Go on," he said, after a moment.

"Well, I don't necessarily mean to do with anyone *at* the theatre. Anyone who works there, I mean. But it was the timing of it that made me pause. I mean, it was a very dramatic play and we were all mesmerised by it. I don't think I would have noticed anything going on around me in the seats. Well, I *didn't* notice anything, apart from the woman that came in right before the play started. Once the play had started, I might have been in another world. So you see, sir, it was a very good place for the murderer to strike, because nobody was taking any notice of them." I subsided, gripping my cooling tea-cup with both hands. I hoped it hadn't sounded as though I was implying Inspector Marks didn't know his job.

"That's very interesting," Inspector Marks said. I breathed an inner sigh of relief. "That's very interesting indeed, Joan. Thank you." After another brief silence he went on. "Your friend, Miss Hunter

– her uncle is one of the actors at the theatre, isn't he?"

"Yes, Tommy – I mean Mister Vance – is Verity's uncle. That's why we were able to see the play – he'd arranged for free tickets."

"Hmm." The inspector drained his cup and put it back on the kitchen table. "I suppose you girls know the actors and the crew quite well?"

"Well, Verity more so than me," I confessed. "But we're going back there on Tuesday to see the play – the whole of it, I mean, this time. Unless anybody else gets killed." I laughed a completely brainless laugh after I said this and the inspector smiled minutely but didn't laugh in response. I could feel the surging tide of blood in my cheeks at my stupidity. "I'm sorry, I mean – I'm sure nothing like that will happen." I still tinkled a laugh on the end of this sentence. *Hold your tongue, Joan.*

"So you ladies will be going backstage, after the play?" The inspector sounded quite casual but there was just a shade of something in his voice, something that made me forget my blushes and my silly girlish giggling and meet his eye.

"That's right," I said slowly. "We'll get to meet everyone then. I hope."

"I understand," said Inspector Marks. We continued to hold each other's gaze for a moment. It was as if he was trying to tell me something telepathically. But what? Was he – was he giving me permission to try and *investigate* what happened?

For a moment, I was sure that he was, and then his gaze dropped and he got up from the table, brushing his hands together to remove the biscuit crumbs. Quickly, I leapt to my feet too.

"Do let me know if you hear anything interesting, Miss Hart. Joan."

"I will, sir."

For a moment I thought he was going to shake my hand but he obviously thought better of it. He nodded again, with a rather embarrassed smile, and then he was gone.

Chapter Eight

IT WAS VERY ODD TO be back in the theatre again, up in the Gods again. At least we didn't have to sit in the same seats again – that would have been a little too close to the memory of the night of the murder for comfort. The seat where the man had been killed had been removed, as had several feet of the dusty red carpet around it. I suppose it had been too stained to be used again, and who on Earth would have bought a ticket for *that* particular seat, even at a penny a go? They wouldn't have been able to give that seat away.

We were the only ones in the Gods that performance. I suppose it wasn't usually a very busy night, a Tuesday evening during the middle of the play's run, but I would have expected at least a few other playgoers to have joined us by the time the curtain went up.

"Too scared," Verity said, leaning back in her seat a trifle smugly. "They think they're going to fall victim to the dastardly seat stabber of nineteen thirty two."

"Oh, don't," I said, more nervously than I meant to. I glanced at the sea of empty seats around us. What if somebody was hiding behind them? You're being fanciful, I told myself but I still had to get up and take a quick look, just to check. Verity watched me with an amused smile.

"I've already done that," she said. "While you went to the Ladies."

I couldn't help but smile. "Ah, so you're just as nervy as I am then."

Verity snorted and then gestured for me to sit down. "Come on, it's starting. We'll be alright." I sat back down and took off my cardigan; it got hot up here in the Gods. Verity added "Besides, now that we're here all alone, it's like our own private box."

I smiled and tried to dismiss my anxiety. Of course, as soon as the play started, I forgot my nerves. Once more I was riveted by Caroline Carpenter's performance. She was the first one to appear on stage – in fact, she was in almost every scene in the first act. Tommy and she had a wonderful sparring of wits in the first scene, which was both exciting and comical. I watched out for Aldous Smith, wondering if he would be much different from that first time I'd seen him. When he appeared in the second scene, I could see he was a little more relaxed on the stage, a little more convincing than he had been the first time we'd seen the show.

As we applauded the stage as the interval curtain went down and the massive chandelier hanging from the auditorium's ceiling glowed back to life, I couldn't help a nervous glance over to where the body had been found. Of course, there was nothing there, not even the chair he'd been sitting on.

Verity rummaged in her handbag and produced her purse with an air of triumph. She waved it at me. "Got enough for a couple of ices, Joan. What do you say?"

"Ooh, yes please." A refreshment at the theatre was a rare luxury, but Verity earned more than I did so I was happy for her to treat me occasionally.

"Come on, then."

The Gods didn't have its own bar. We had to walk down a flight of steps to the bar that served the Dress Circle. It wasn't very busy, unusually so for an interval. I wondered whether the murder had scared off the public and said as much to Verity.

"Maybe," she said, rather cynically. "I would have thought the great British public would have flocked to the scene of a murder, just to gawk at where it happened. I thought Tommy said they had sold out for the next few weeks."

Remembering the public furore over the Asharton Manor murders and the Merisham Lodge case, I had to agree. Perhaps it was just that it was mid-week and the cold and rainy night was discouraging people.

"I suppose it's lucky that they didn't have to cancel the entire run," I said, as we found seats by the back of the bar and ate our ices.

"Yes, that's exactly what Tommy was saying." Verity licked her little spoon with relish. "He was frantic that the whole show was going to be cancelled and he was going to be out of work."

"Will we see him afterwards?"

"Of course." She paused and gave me rather a sly look sideways. "You're rather keen on our Tommy, aren't you, Joanie?"

"I am not!" I said, hotly. "I just think he's a nice man, that's all."

"Oh he is, he's lovely. But you know, Joanie, he's not for you. He's not that way inclined, if you see what I mean."

Of course I knew what she meant. Did she think I was stupid or something? I said nothing but gave her a look, and then a poke with my ice-cream spoon for good measure, and she ducked away, laughing. The bell rang to remind us to retake our seats.

As we walked back to the Gods, up the stairs, I took note of the entrance. There was a small landing at the top of the steps, with a narrow corridor leading to the lavatories for this floor. The steps led down to the bar in which we'd just been and then onwards, down to the Grand Circle and finally to the stalls on the ground floor of the auditorium. As I walked into the Gods, I tried to think like the murderer would have. Had it been that woman I'd seen or someone else who'd crept in after dark? But then, how had the man been stabbed through the back of the chair if the woman had sat there and she *hadn't* been the killer? I looked around, searching for another entrance, a hidden door or something like that, and even got up and walked about along the back row of seats, looking harder, but there was nothing. Just a plain, unbroken wall. There was no possible way that the killer could have climbed down into the Gods by the balcony without having been seen by Tophat and his group of friends, so the murderer must have come up via the staircase. But then, why had nobody seen him – or her?

"Come on, Joan, it's starting," Verity whispered, and I sat back down in my seat and turned my attention towards the play.

I enjoyed the second act even more than I had the first. Caroline's character, of course, ending up renouncing the bad boy (Tommy) for the good man (Aldous) but the way the playwright went about it meant that Verity and I were on the edge of our seats to see which way the leading lady would take. When the final applause finally died down, Verity and I looked at one another with rather dazed delight.

"She's awfully good, isn't she? Caroline Car-penter, I mean." I began to gather up my things in preparation for our departure.

"Yes she is. Come on, let's give it five minutes and then we'll go down and meet everyone."

We retired to the Ladies' Room to powder our noses, renew our lipstick and repair our hairstyles. Fighting to get mine back into its rapidly drooping pin curls, I made a vow that I would cut my hair, cut it really short. Just think how much cooler it would be in the kitchen, I thought to myself, thrusting in the last errant hairpin with a vengeance.

I hadn't been backstage at this theatre before. The backstage door was at the back of the ground floor, around behind a partition. Verity knocked and the door was opened by a young woman who I didn't know but Verity did, judging by the warm welcome she received.

"Verity! You're here. Come through and I'll hunt out Tommy for you."

Verity introduced me. "This is my friend, Miss Joan Hart. Joan, this is Gwen Deeds. She's the wardrobe mistress here."

I shook hands with Gwen. She had a round, cheerful face and was about my height, so fairly tall for a woman. She wasn't pretty but she had nice, kind, brown eyes, as placid as a cow's. She greeted me with warmth and bade us to come backstage again.

As always, I was slightly unprepared for the change in tempo. Out in the auditorium, there was the subdued buzz of excitement and anticipation.

Here, backstage, it was bedlam. Stage hands clomped past with bits of the scenery, props girls rushed back and forth with chairs and candlesticks and potted plants, various musicians carried their instruments (Verity murmured that they would soon be out from under our feet and off to the pub) and of course, there were the actors. It was a small cast for this particular play but actors have a way of filling up the space, no matter how many of them there are.

We came out into the main room at the back and spotted Tommy, his dyed hair gleaming under the lights. He was talking to Aldous, who was looking rather flushed, something that made him even more attractive. Both of them had cloths in their hands and were occupied in cleaning the greasepaint from their faces, even as they were talking nineteen to the dozen.

We struggled across the crowded floor (I had to avert my eyes a couple of times from several men who were still dressing) and Tommy spotted us as we got closer. He swept Verity into a hug and planted a kiss on my cheek. I tried not to blush and also tried not to raise my hand to see if he'd smeared greasepaint all over my face.

"Well, my darlings, what did you think?"

Of course we said, quite honestly, that the play had been marvellous, and he had been marvellous and so, of course, had Aldous and Miss Carpenter.

Aldous smiled when we mentioned his name. He seemed a little more relaxed than when we had last met, a little less strange and awkward. Looking at both Tommy and he, I could see they were both experiencing the euphoria I'd seen before in actors who'd just come off the stage. A sort of mixture of relief, giddiness, and perhaps a tinge of melancholy that it was all over. For a moment, I felt envious. When did I ever get to feel like that in my job?

A door at the back of the room opened, a door with a golden star painted on the front of it. Caroline Carpenter appeared in the doorway's empty frame, a languid vision in a cream silk dressing gown, an ebony cigarette holder in one hand. I saw her gaze move about the room until it rested on Tommy and Aldous.

Aldous looked up at the same time, as if his gaze was subtly attuned to Caroline's. Caroline made a beckoning gesture, and as Aldous moved forward, she called out, "Tommy, darling, I need you in here." The way Aldous' face fell was almost amusing. Caroline must have relented because she said "Oh, and you too, Aldous. And, Verity Hunter, is that you? Why don't you bring your little friend in for champagne?"

Verity and I looked at one another and moved as one towards Caroline's dressing room. Champagne! I had never tasted it before, and the chance to drink some with a famous actress – fairly famous, at least – was not one to be passed up lightly.

Chapter Nine

IF I COULD HAVE DESCRIBED the inside of Caroline Carpenter's dressing room in one word, I think I would have chosen 'exotic'. I mentioned this to Verity on the way home and she'd chuckled in a dirty manner and said, "I think mine would have been 'bordello'," which made both of us laugh very loudly. Anyway, it was very plush, with lots of red velvet and gilt and with a chaise-longue in crimson silk, a chandelier hanging from the ceiling that was a tiny baby of the one in the main auditorium. An enormous dressing table was filled from side to side with boxes and pots and bags, and electric lightbulbs framed around the edge of the enormous mirror. It was like being in something from Arabian Nights.

Verity and I sat down rather self-consciously on two low stools. Caroline lay back on the chaise-longue, modestly arranging the cream silk of her dressing gown to cover her legs. She had a pair of the most elegant, gold, high-heeled shoes on and her toenails were painted bright scarlet. Dorothy would have been green with envy. The engagement ring on Caroline's finger caught the light from the chandelier and flashed like fire.

"So, my darlings, weren't we just wonderful? Aldous, do the honours, will you?" Caroline gestured to the silver ice bucket that stood on a small table behind the chaise-longue.

She and Tommy began a spirited discussion about their respective performances. I listened to them whilst watching Aldous open the champagne, which he did fairly dextrously. There was still a loud bang and Caroline shrieked as the cork ricocheted off the ceiling, narrowly missing the chandelier.

"My God, darling, mind the glass. That's all we need, to be killed by a plummeting chandelier."

"That's right," Tommy said, gaily. "We've only just seen the last of the police as it is."

Verity and I exchanged glances. "They'd been questioning you all, then?" Verity asked.

Caroline put a hand to her chest and rolled her beautiful green eyes. "Every day they've been here, asking their questions and poking about in corners. It was a real distraction, wasn't it, Aldous?" She bestowed him with a dazzling smile as he handed her a glass of champagne, beaded with condensation.

He didn't reply as such but muttered something with his head down, suddenly returning to the rather sulky young man we'd met before. He remembered his manners though and fetched a glass for Verity and myself which we took with eager gratitude.

As Caroline went on to elaborate the myriad annoyances of the police presence, I took a tentative sip of champagne. The bubbles went straight up my nose and I had to quickly stop myself from sneezing. What an unsophisticated idiot. Luckily, nobody had seen my *faux-pas*. They were still listening to Caroline and Tommy, who was chipping in with his own experiences.

"Of course, I told them I'd never seen this mysterious woman, I was on stage for half the first act. In fact, it was just before we were due to go back on stage for Act Two that David came running in, white as a ghost – you remember, Caroline – and said the show has to stop—"

"I was just astonished," said Caroline. I got the feeling that they had discussed this many times before and that their respective parts of the conversation had solidified from subjective observation to fact. "Just *astonished*. It was—"

"Come on, darling, you were more than *astonished*. You were virtually prostrated, once they told us about the murder."

Caroline fluttered her left hand and the ring winked and flashed in the light from above. "I was still caught up in the play, darling, that's all. I was in a highly vulnerable emotional state. Mind you, it did give us all a turn, didn't it? There was David, practically having a fit, the poor man, and the scene hands all for turning out and hunting down the killer—"

"Until the police turned up and told them not to," chipped in Tommy.

"And the musicians completely oblivious until they were told they couldn't go and get drunk, and the backstage girls screaming and fainting – oh, my goodness, it was a *circus*." I noticed Caroline had already drained her glass and at that moment she held it out wordlessly to Aldous. He took it and refilled it without comment. I'd barely drunk any of mine – for something I'd looked forward to for so long, it was a bit of a disappointment, actually. I preferred half an ale.

Caroline was still speaking. Even off stage, she had a way of keeping her audience spellbound. I wasn't sure if it was her beauty or the intonation in her voice that kept us riveted. "Anyway, I saw in the paper today, they've finally identified the body. Aldous, be a darling—" She clicked her fingers and pointed towards the dressing table. "Bring me the paper, would you? Oh, thank you so much. Look, look here. He was Italian, apparently. Guido Bonsignore was his name."

"Italian?" I exclaimed, and everybody looked at me. It was the first time I'd spoken. I fought not to blush and cleared my throat. "I'm sorry, it's just that that's interesting in the light of how he was killed, don't you think?"

Everyone was still staring at me, Verity and Tommy in a receptive way, Caroline in a sort of amazement at somebody like me having a voice and Aldous with a blank, vacant stare. I cleared my throat again and mumbled something about the fact that he'd been killed in a way that the police thought might have been a professional murder.

"Oh, a *gang* killing you mean?" Caroline said eventually, when the silence after my remark had stretched on into infinity. She sounded politely incredulous. "Because he was Italian? I suppose that's possible."

"You mean he was a Mafioso, Joan?" asked Tommy. He smiled at me, kindly. "Have the police said that?"

"No, no, I didn't mean that," I said, stuttering a little. I could see Caroline looking at me and thought I could read her mind. What on Earth would the police be doing talking to someone like me? "I just meant that it's a possibility, that's all. Like Miss Carpenter says." I threw her a respectful smile, which was not returned.

There was a moment of silence and then Caroline snapped her gaze away from me, dismissal evident in the movement. "Well," she said, "*I* think—" but we never got to find out what she thought because right then there was a knock at the door.

"Come in," Caroline called languidly. She'd finished the second glass of champagne. The door opened and a bunch of roses bigger than a small child entered. Hidden behind them, one of the stage hands said respectfully, "Sir Nicolas Holmes is here, Miss Carpenter."

Caroline sat up straighter and put the champagne flute down on the floor. "How wonderful. Put the flowers over there, John, thank you. You may go."

A man's figure loomed in the doorway after John had left and a moment later was in the room. He was tall and portly, much older than I had imagined, fifty if he was a day. His grey hair matched his bushy grey moustache and he wore full evening dress. I saw his gaze flick around the room in astonishment before coming to rest on Caroline, which was when he smiled.

"My dear," he said, coming further forward and taking off his hat. "You were no doubt as superb as usual tonight. I'm so sorry I couldn't be here to watch you – a late sitting in the House, you know."

"That's perfectly all right, darling." Caroline got up, smiling. The rest of us scrambled to our feet too. The room felt very crowded, and I wasn't surprised when Caroline said to the air in general, "My fiancé, Sir Nicolas Holmes, Member of Parliament. You really must excuse us." She didn't bother to introduce the rest of us, and it was clear we were expected to go. Tommy and Aldous had a wintry smile bestowed upon them by Sir Nicolas, but Verity and I were completely ignored. As we filed out, just about tugging our forelocks in an attempt to convey respect, I was reminded irresistibly of Lord Cartwright. Was there a factory somewhere in England turning out these old, fat, moustached aristocrats?

The door to Caroline's room shut firmly behind us. Aldous muttered something to us – I suppose it could have been 'goodbye' – and sloped off. Tommy put his arm around Verity and gave her a squeeze.

"Well, that was the big man himself. Bit of a cold fish, eh?"

Verity rolled her eyes. "He was exactly as I pictured him."

"What does Caroline see in him?" I asked, honestly curious as to why someone with so much talent, vivacity and beauty would want to marry someone so devoid of all those qualities.

Tommy and Verity laughed out loud. "What, apart from the fact he owns half of Northamptonshire?" said Tommy.

"And he can trace his family name back to the Domesday Book?" said Verity.

"All right, all right," I said, half laughing, half annoyed. "But money and breeding isn't everything."

Verity grew serious. "Money *is* everything – to some people."

Tommy glanced at his watch. "Now, can I take

you lovely ladies out for dinner somewhere? Or do you have to get back?"

Verity grinned with glee. "We're free for the whole evening. Well, as long as we're back at eleven o'clock."

"Good God, Verity, that gives me half an hour to feed you, if that's the case. You still have to catch the train home."

I drooped a little. I would have so loved to have gone out to dinner with Tommy and Verity, my two favourite people in the world.

Tommy must have noticed my dejection. He gave me a squeeze too. "Cheer up, Joan. I'm sure we can manage pie and mash somewhere." He took another glance at his watch. "Lord, only if we hurry though. Come on, there's a place just around the corner."

Verity and I didn't need telling twice. We bundled ourselves into our coats and hats and hurried after Tommy as he led the way out of the theatre.

THE PIE AND MASH SHOP was hot and crowded and noisy. Tommy went off to battle his way to the counter to order our food, and Verity and I tried to find a table to sit at. As we struggled through the heaving mass of bodies in the shop, there was a call and an arm waving to us from a table at the back. It was Gwen Deeds, the wardrobe mistress from the theatre, perched up on one of the benches with a steaming plate of food in front of her.

"Verity! Over here. Come on, quick, while these seats are free."

Verity shouted over to Tommy to tell him where we were going and then we forged a path as best we could through to Gwen.

"Phew," Verity gasped, finally making it to a seat. "This place is a mad house."

"I know," Gwen said cheerfully. She made a space for us to put our coats, which we definitely did not need in there. I could feel the sweat beginning to trickle down my back. "Half the theatre folk around here come in here after the shows."

I curiously looked around me at my fellow diners. I recognised a couple of people from the Connault Theatre by sight and wondered if we'd see Aldous Smith, though I couldn't spot him in the crowd.

Tommy came through the press of people with a tray in his hands and the air of a man who had fought a long, hard battle. "Bloody hell, it gets worse every night. Here you go, ladies." He handed around plates of pie and mash and a glass of ale for us all. "Chin-chin."

We clinked glasses and set to with a will, Verity and I conscious of the fact that we had very little time before we had to leave. Gwen, having started eating before us, had more time for talking, and she and Tommy began discussing Sir Nicolas Holmes with avidity.

"Rich as Croesus, he is," said Gwen. Her round red cheeks shone in the heat. "One of the most eligible bachelors in London and Miss Caroline managed to snag him."

"Well, good for her," said Tommy, swilling his ale. "We've got to make our own luck in this world. Wish *I* had that option." Verity and I exchanged glances and guiltily lowered our smiles to our plates.

"Do you know when the wedding is?" Gwen asked.

"Not for some time. You know what it's going to be like; white silk to the rafters, orange blossom, gilded carriages, probably. White doves."

"Do you think she'll carry on acting after she's married?"

"She'll have to," I exclaimed. "She couldn't possibly stop acting, surely, just because she's married. It would be criminal to waste that talent."

Gwen shrugged. "She may not have a choice. You know, once the babies come and all that."

She looked thoughtful for a moment and then said "She's lucky. *She* gets a choice."

There was bitterness in her tone. I wondered if it was because she'd like to get married herself and knew there was little chance of that. Well, I knew just how she felt.

"Being wardrobe mistress must be very interesting," I said, wanting to cheer her up a bit. I didn't know her from Adam but she seemed a nice girl, and I didn't like seeing her sad.

It was the right thing to say. Gwen brightened and said, "Oh, it is! I love it. I love fashion and textiles, and it's wonderful when you have a chance to really make a difference to a play, you know, in making sure the costumes are just right."

She went on in the same vein for a little while, her affection for her job quite apparent. Again, I felt envious. Just like the actors, Gwen was following a passion and being paid for it. Was I ever going to get the chance to do something similar? I loved writing, and the theatre, and I thought I had a little talent for it. But who was ever going to pay me to write stories and plays? I didn't even know where to begin.

That evening, over a plate of pie and mash, I made a resolution. I would begin to find out about writing professionally – if it was even possible for someone like me to do such a thing. *You only live once, Joan.*

"It must have its downsides," I said to Gwen, thinking that I had better be realistic about my ambitions.

"Oh, yes, of course. The way some of the actors treat the costumes is just shocking. Rips and stains... I'm up half the night mending them, sometimes, so they'll be ready for the show. *And—*" she went on, in a darker tone, "sometimes things go *missing*, if you see what I mean."

"Stolen?" I asked in a suitably shocked tone.

"Well, I wouldn't like to use *that* word out loud, but yes, it does happen. Only a week ago or so I had a whole costume disappear. I thought I'd mislaid it, but perhaps someone came along and pinched it—"

She was interrupted by Verity's urgent summons. "Joan, it's five and twenty past ten. We *have* to go."

"Yes, we must." I smiled at Gwen and shook her hand. "It was so nice to meet you, Gwen."

"And you too. You and Verity must come and have tea with me someday."

"I would like that very much. Goodbye, Tommy, and thanks so much for the meal."

Tommy kissed us both. "You're very welcome, my darlings. Glad you liked the play. I've got an audition for pantomime next week so who knows? You might be able to come and watch me in that too, after this run finishes."

"It might go on for much longer," Verity said, giving him a hug. "You three are so good in it, it deserves to be seen by everyone."

We said goodbye once more and battled our way out to the street. Running for the underground on a full stomach wasn't very comfortable but it had to be done. We pelted down the steps, down the escalators, across the platform and into a waiting train, just as the conductor was about to clash the metal gate closed. He gave us a disapproving look but we took no notice, casting ourselves upon the seats, hardly able to speak for laughing.

Chapter Ten

IT WAS TOO LATE BY the time Verity and I got home to have a proper read of the article about the dead man, now identified as Guido Bonsignore. The first thing I did the next morning, as soon as I was able to take a break from work, was to snatch up the paper and sit down to read that article word for word. Not that it was a particularly long article. The story had already moved off the front page – news doesn't last long in London, even that of a brutal murder. Guido Bonsignore had apparently lived in a rooming house in Victoria, but the police believed he had only been in the country for six months or so. There was no mention of the fact that he may have been using a false name. Surely Inspector Marks had mentioned that to me? Or had I imagined it? Why would he have told *me* and yet the papers be unaware of it? I read again the sentence which mentioned the dead man's lodgings. He had lived in a rooming house in Ashbourne Grove, Victoria. Would it be worth going there to see if I could find anything out? Surely the police would have thoroughly searched the place by now. What on Earth did I think I could find that specially trained officers couldn't?

"Well, Joan," Mrs Watling said, bustling in and making me jump, so engrossed had I been in reading about the murder victim. "We've got something a bit different tonight. Her ladyship is hosting a cocktail party, so there won't be a dinner as such, but there'll be a lot of *hors d'oeuvres*, some light dishes and so forth. They're not as much work as a full dinner but they take more time because of all the fiddling about, so we'd better get started right away."

I shook myself back to reality and put the paper to one side. "What about the cocktails, Mrs Watling?"

"Oh, don't you worry about that. Mr Fenwick will deal with the drinks, and I think her ladyship has a cocktail bartender coming in specially."

I raised my eyebrows but said nothing. Mrs Watling sat down at the kitchen table and began dashing off a list of increasingly complicated *amuse-bouches*. She looked up at me, her brow creased in consternation. "Caviar, Joan. We must have some caviar."

"I'll ring the fishmonger," I said. Making my way into the hallway in search of the telephone, I met Verity, who was just coming down the stairs.

"Morning, Joanie," she said with a yawn.

"I don't know what you're yawning for," I said a

little grumpily. "I'm the one who should be yawning. You were snoring away when I left this morning."

"Got out of the wrong side of bed this morning, did we?" She gave me a poke in the ribs and I laughed, despite myself.

"Listen," I said, drawing her to one side. "Did you read the article about the man – you know, the man at the theatre?"

"Not yet."

I gave her the *precis* of the article. "His boarding house was in Victoria. I was thinking of going there on my next afternoon off, see if there was anything to find."

Verity looked at me with her eyebrows quirked. "Joanie—" She hesitated and then said, "Well, it's up to you, of course. But don't you think the police will have found out anything there is to be found?"

Despite me having those exact thoughts just half an hour earlier, I was still a little stung. "It was only an idea," I muttered defensively.

"Well, it's up to you. I can think of nicer places to go on my afternoon off. When *is* your next afternoon off?"

"Saturday. Dorothy normally dines out on Saturday, doesn't she?"

Verity nodded. "Normally. She's having a shindig tonight, did you know? Well I suppose you do. Look, I've got the guest list here." She dug in her dress pocket and flourished a piece of paper at me.

I took it and read it curiously. Most of the names meant nothing to me apart from a few of Dorothy's old friends. But there was one name on there that made me suck in my breath.

"What is it?" asked Verity.

"Look. The Honourable Cleo Maddox." I pointed to the name with a finger that was not quite steady. Verity looked blank. "She was Delphine Denford's friend. You know, at Asharton Manor."

The name of the Manor had its usual effect on Verity. She blinked and recoiled slightly. "Talk about the past coming back to haunt you," she murmured, and we both looked at Cleo Maddox's name in silence, which was broken by Mrs Watling's shout from the kitchen.

"Joan! I need you."

"Oh, blast, I need to call the fishmonger. Here, take this back." I thrust the paper back at Verity and ran for the telephone.

ONCE BACK IN THE KITCHEN, and chopping away industriously, I let my thoughts drift back to the Honourable Cleo Maddox and the place where I'd first encountered her, Asharton Manor. The first place where Verity and I had become involved in solving a crime. By now, the fishmonger's boy had brought a crate of smoked salmon, shrimp and caviar, all packed in ice, and I dipped into it and removed the ingredients I needed, wincing at the pain in my freezing fingers. The smoked salmon and cream cheese pinwheels were the very devil to roll up. Eventually I managed it and affixed each one with a toothpick. I must say, I was quite surprised that Cleo Maddox hadn't married by now. She, like Dorothy, was rich, high-born and beautiful. Perhaps, like Dorothy, the events of the recent past had put her off the idea of matrimony.

The hustle and bustle of the morning's work had driven the thought of Guido Bonsignore from my mind. While I was helping Doris clear the servants' hall after luncheon, I began thinking of him again. Why was I so determined to find out what had happened? There were plenty of murders in London that I had not the slightest interest in, or the desire to solve the mystery of who had committed them. Was it because I'd actually been there and hadn't seen the killer? Or hadn't seen the killer well enough to identify them? But how could I have seen them properly? The darkness of the theatre had been an effective disguise.

I stopped, with a dirty plate in my hand. Just then there had been a moment; a quicksilver flash in my brain, of *something* – something important. I strained after it, trying to recall the thought but, frustratingly, it was gone. What had it been?

"Can I 'ave that plate, Joan?"

I brought myself back to reality and handed

Doris the piece of crockery. No matter. Surely if what I had thought was important, it would come back to me.

DOROTHY'S COCKTAIL PARTY BEGAN AT eight o'clock. Because there hadn't been a full meal to prepare, the servants were able to sit down to a more leisurely evening meal than they would normally have had. Only poor Andrew, Mr Fenwick and Nancy had to remain upstairs to cater to every whim of the guests. For Nancy the pain was lessened, it appeared, by being able to remain in the vicinity of the temporary cocktail barman, who apparently could have been the double of Rudolf Valentino. She told us this, with much fluttering of the hands and rolling of her eyes, when she came down for some extra dishes.

"You should see him, Joan. Eyes like coals, and he's got one of those warm deep voices that just makes you melt..."

"Really?" I said in a non-committal sort of tone, but funnily enough, both Doris and I volunteered to help her carry some of the dishes back up the stairs so we could catch a glimpse of this Adonis.

The person who first caught my eye when I sidled into the drawing room was not the bartender, however. It was Cleo Maddox, standing over by the far wall in a beautiful dress of peacock blue satin, with shimmering gold tassels that edged the neckline and were arranged in tiers over the skirt. She wore a gold band in her black hair, which was still cut in the geometric flapper bob that it had been at Asharton Manor. She looked older, though; beautiful, as ever, but older, harder, her eyes ringed in dark shadow.

There was an awkward moment when our eyes met; she must have sensed me staring at her from across the room. There was a flash of – not recognition, exactly, but something – and then she snapped her gaze away from mine as if I weren't there.

Feeling hot in the face, I carried the dish of *hors d'oeuvres* over to the table where the other food was set. After a cursory glance at the bartender – he was good looking enough, I supposed, but not really my type – I collected Doris and we made our way back downstairs, leaving the cigarette smoke, the alcohol fumes, and the brittle, drunken laughter behind us.

Chapter Eleven

THE WEEK ROLLED ON UNEVENTFULLY. The usual routine of work continued; preparing meals, serving meals, clearing up after the meals, and ordering the next day's food. After Dorothy's cocktail party there were no other big meals to prepare for a while. Apparently, according to Verity, Dorothy had to spend the entire next day in bed recovering after her shindig, so she obviously didn't feel up to any more entertaining at the moment. By Friday night she'd recovered enough to dine out, which made for a nice, relaxed evening for me and Mrs Watling.

The only other moment of note was on Friday morning, when Tommy called round to tell Verity that he'd got the pantomime role. Pleased as punch, he was, and of course, we had to invite him in and toast his success with a good pot of coffee and some of the fresh-baked scones Mrs Watling had prepared that morning.

"But what about *Voyage of the Heart*?" I asked. "I thought that was due to run up to Christmas?"

Tommy shook his head, his face rueful. "They're shutting it down early. The crowds are falling off and the backers are worried it's going to end up being a flop after all."

"It can't be," exclaimed Verity. "You've had wonderful reviews. You all have." She meant Caroline and Aldous as well as Tommy.

"I know. And believe me, it's going to stand me in good stead. But you know what an actor's life is, Verity. It's the constant uncertainty as to whether you'll be able to eat and pay the rent at the end of every month." Tommy drained his coffee cup and put the cup back on the table. "I don't blame Caroline for getting out while the going's good. I'd do the same myself, if I could."

Mrs Watling looked a little bit mystified by this part of the conversation. Biting back a giggle, I congratulated Tommy once more on landing the new part in the pantomime. "You're not playing the Dame, are you?" I asked and then blushed because that sounded rather...pointed.

Tommy laughed out loud. "No, not me. I'm Buttons, faithful side-kick to Cinderella. You and Verity will have to come and see me."

"I'd love that," I said, and Verity added her agreement.

THE NEXT DAY WAS SATURDAY and I had my afternoon off to look forward to. Sometimes, Verity and I were able to coordinate our afternoons so that we could spend our time off together, but it didn't always work like that and today was one of those days. Verity was accompanying Dorothy to a fashion parade in the West End and wouldn't be back until quite late. Putting away the last few dishes after luncheon, I wondered how to spend my precious free time. Should I go and see a motion picture? Or perhaps visit the book shops of Charing Cross Road – I wouldn't be able to afford to buy anything but you could get away with reading quite a lot during a browse of the shelves, if you were careful about it. I closed the door of the dresser, folded the tea towel neatly and hung it over the handle of the range. Perhaps I'd just travel into the centre of London and see where the mood took me. Mrs Watling and Doris had tonight's meal under control, and Dorothy would be dining out again tonight, so I had nothing to hurry back for. What a glorious thought.

I ran upstairs quickly, got changed, re-pinned my hair and affixed my hat to my head. It was quite a good hat, a cloche in a lovely dark red velvet, one of Dorothy's cast-offs which she'd passed to Verity, who'd passed it to me. As I regarded myself in the small mirror that hung over the dressing table, I felt, for a change, quite satisfied with my appearance. My coat was old but I'd pressed it and starched the collar so it looked quite smart, my gloves were fairly new (a birthday present from Verity) and the hat's colour suited my dark hair. I dabbed my face with powder, touched up my lips and took up my handbag.

For late autumn, it was a lovely day; bright and fresh with the sun shining from a clear blue sky. Not warm though and you could feel the chill of winter in the breeze. I had been going to take an omnibus but I decided against it and made my way to the nearest Underground station, where it would be smoky and steamy but would at least be warm.

A kind man offered me his seat and I took it with a grateful smile. Then, because he showed slightly worrying signs of wanting to flirt with me, I quickly unfolded the paper I'd picked up at the entrance to the tube and opened it up, shielding my face from his attention.

As always, I looked for more news about the theatre murder, or even about Lord Cartwright, but on both accounts there was nothing, although I read the paper from cover to cover. I was soon so absorbed that I forgot both the man hovering over me and the fact that I'd meant to alight the train at Oxford Circus. I looked up from the back page of the newspaper with a start to realise that the train had passed through the centre of London and was now approaching Victoria. *Victoria*... That was where Guido Bonsignore had lived in his rooming house.

Acting on impulse, I leapt from my seat as the

train drew into the station, and before I knew it, I was out on the platform and walking up the stairs to the main train station and the exit. I came out into the open air, feeling rather breathless at my daring. Because I was – yes, I really was – going to find his rooming house and see if I could have a look around.

I didn't have a map on me but after asking several passersby for directions, I found myself in Ashbourne Grove, a rather down-at-heel road lined on either side with tall, drab houses. You could see that they had once been very grand residences, but now the paint was peeling from their exteriors, the windows were grimy or on occasion broken, and the pavement was littered with rubbish. I walked slowly and nervously up the street until I came to number 81, the rooming house where Guido Bonsignore had lived.

I don't know what I expected – to see a crowd of police outside, perhaps or some gawking onlookers. There was nothing like that, just a defeated looking old man shuffling down the steps from the tatty front door. He passed me without a glance as I climbed the steps, feeling more jittery with every one I climbed.

Faced with the solidly shut front door, I hesitated. Then I reached out and rang the doorbell marked 'Management'. I could hear it chime on the other side and I waited, not really knowing what I was doing.

After a wait of what seemed like hours, but was probably only five minutes, the door opened and a hard-faced, pinched-mouthed woman stood there, in a grubby overall, with a look of deep suspicion on her face. She looked me up and down properly before snapping out, "Yes?"

"Um – I was wondering—" It was only now I realised how silly I was not to have thought up a good story as to why I wanted to get into the house. "Um – I'm looking for a room."

I got the up-and-down glance again. "Oh, you are, are you? And who might you be?"

"My name's Gladys Smith," I said quite firmly, surprising myself. "I'm a typist at a bureau in Victoria and I need to find new accommodation. Is there a room free?"

The woman sniffed. "I don't normally 'ave young ladies rooming here. Just men."

"Oh." I was stumped for a second. Then I rallied. "Well, perhaps I could come in and have a look? I've got good references, and I can pay the first month's rent upfront."

That had an effect. The woman, whilst still wearing a frown of deep suspicion, sniffed again and then, after a moment, stood back a little, pulling the door a little wider. "Well, I don't know as this is the sort of place for you, but I suppose you can come in and 'ave a look. Just for a moment, mind."

"Thank you." I tried to sound suitably grateful. I stepped forward and into a dark, cluttered hallway where my nostrils were assailed with the mingled scents of boiled cabbage, stale beer and unwashed socks. Possibly unemptied chamberpots as well. Trying not to breathe, I followed the old harridan up the narrow flight of stairs.

"I heard that room twelve was empty," I gasped as we got to the first floor. That was a mistake.

The woman swung round to face me, suspicion etched ever deeper on her already heavily lined face. "'Ere, what's the story? That's that bloke's room, that geezer who was murdered. What d'you want with that one?"

"Nothing," I stuttered. "I just heard it was free, that's all."

The woman swore. She leant forward, peering at me through the dimness of the corridor. "You a journalist? Poking your nose in here when it's not wanted? This is a respectable 'ouse, nothing like what the papers reported. Go on, get on out of it. I don't know why I fell for it in the first place."

Although I'd been a servant for my whole working life, I wasn't used to people being so nakedly aggressive towards me. I tried to stand my ground, stammering out something about not being a journalist, but the woman came towards me, actually shaking her fist.

"Go on, get out! Bloody parasites, coming round 'ere and poking your nose in. I din't know him, you 'ere me? I din't know him from Adam, so you're wasting your time. Go on, out with yer!"

Shaken, I hurried back down the stairs and out through the front door, the woman's admonishments following me and growing fainter as I shut the front door hurriedly behind me. I almost fell down the steps, so desperate was I to get away. Oh dear, what a mess I'd made of it. I hoped the landlady wasn't even now calling the police. Now, she wouldn't do that, surely? Hurriedly I walked back out into the street and paused for breath. The smoky air of Victoria tasted quite fresh after the miasma I'd encountered in that rooming house. I wasn't much of a private detective, really, was I, turning tail and running away at the first bit of opposition I encountered...

I was still too shaken by my recent experience to realise that someone was hovering right behind my shoulder, waiting for my attention. Nerves singing, I whirled around, expecting it to be the landlady, ready to give me a walloping but to my great relief, it was a slovenly sort of girl, probably no older than seventeen, dressed in a dirty overall and eyeing me with mingled fascination and dislike.

"Got a light?" was all she said.

I always carry a box of matches around with me

in my handbag – they come in handy more times than you might think. I nodded, bringing myself back under control and struck a match for her to light her cigarette.

She took a deep drag for a second and the smoke hung in the cold air like a wavering blue scarf before dissolving away. The girl jerked her head towards the house.

"Sent you packing with a flea in your ear, did she?"

I smiled ruefully. "I'm afraid so."

"You a reporter?"

I opened my mouth to say 'no' and found myself saying 'yes' instead. "Yes, that's right. I'm freelance. Why, do you have something to tell me?"

The girl eyed me again. "Any dosh in it? I tried to talk to some of the others who came, after that Guido was killed, but she wouldn't let me talk to any of them, mean old bitch."

I assumed she meant the harridan landlady. "Do you work there, then?" The girl nodded, rolling her eyes. I took a deep breath, assuming, once again, the persona of someone different. "Well, what's your name?"

"Ethel."

"Ethel, can you talk to me now? I mean, will you get into trouble if you come with me now?" Unprepossessing as the girl was, I didn't want to be responsible for her losing her job.

"Nah, I'll be fine. I don't start for another half an hour."

"Well, then." I was going to do this, it seemed. I felt a leap of excitement and anxiety. I wondered if this was how actors felt before they started a performance? "Ethel, I *would* like to talk to you. Is there a good pub somewhere around here we could go to?" I looked around at the rundown street and corrected myself. "I mean, is there a pub around we could go to?"

"Yeah. The Queen's 'Ed, down the end, there."

"Fine. Let's go then. The drinks are on me."

Chapter Twelve

I WALKED INTO THE SALOON BAR of The Queen's Head, feeling as if I was suffering a prolonged bout of madness. What *did* I think I was doing? But then, what if I managed to find something out, something significant? Ethel had worked in the rooming house. From the sounds of it, she'd known Guido Bonsignore. Surely that was worth half an hour of sitting in a rather nasty public house and paying for two halves of ale.

I had never bought a drink for myself in a pub before. I had a nasty moment when I thought the barman wouldn't serve me but they obviously weren't too choosy about their clientele in there. At least in the saloon bar we were less likely to get bothered.

Ethel seemed quite at home here. She'd kept hold of my box of matches when I'd offered them to her and was smoking another cigarette. She fell on the drink I put in front of her as if she were dying of thirst.

"You knew Guido Bonsignore?" I asked her, once she'd come up for air.

Ethel wiped a beer foam moustache from her top lip. "Yeah. I cleaned his room for ''im."

"What was he like?" I asked, properly curious. Despite the fact that I'd actually *seen* his dead body, he'd always seemed rather remote to me, as if he weren't really a real person. But then hadn't Inspector Marks told me that the police thought he was using a false name? Had he *really* said that, or had I just imagined it?

I made an effort to concentrate on what Ethel was saying.

"Yeah, 'e was all right. 'E didn't have much stuff, just an old trunk and a few clothes. Think 'e'd come back from abroad – he wasn't 'alf brown. But then they are, aren't they? Those Italians."

"Did he have an Italian accent?" I could see that Ethel was nearing the end of her drink and wondered if I had enough money to buy her another.

"Well, that's funny, because as far as I could hear, 'e didn't. 'E sounded just like a normal bloke to me. But then 'e must have been an Eye-tie, musn't he? With that name, an' all."

"Did he ever have any visitors?"

Ethel had drained her glass by now and was looking longingly at the dregs at the bottom of the glass. I sighed and said, "Wait here," and went and got her another half. I'd hardly touched my own. It struck me, walking back to the table, that this was an awfully strange way to spend my afternoon off. But it was sort of fun, too, in a way. Pretending to be somebody else.

I repeated my question to Ethel as I sat down and pushed the full glass across the table to her.

"No, 'e never really had no one coming to see 'im. Oh, apart from the lady, one time." That made me sit up.

"The lady? When was this?"

Ethel glugged her beer. "About a month ago, I reckon. I just caught a glimpse of 'er coming out of 'is room. 'Oy, oy,' I thought, 'cos Mrs Smitton don't like any funny business going on, you know what I mean?" I nodded, trying to keep a straight face. "But I don't think anything like that was going on. I don't know – there was something funny about 'er, I thought."

"About this woman?" I checked.

"Yeah, 'er. She come down the corridor and past me but I didn't really get a good look at 'er face. She had a veil on, great big black thing, and a hat pulled right down over 'er face."

"Is there anything else you can tell me about her?" I asked. I felt a twinge of pride – I actually did sound like a real reporter.

Ethel shrugged. "Nothing much else to tell. She was tall. But – I don't know. There was just something funny about 'er."

I pressed her for details but she couldn't or wouldn't elaborate further. By this time, Ethel's second glass was empty and she took a look at the clock up over the bar and swore.

"I'm gonna be late. I've got to go."

"Wait—" I put a hand out to stop her without being sure of what it was I was going to say. I didn't want to give her my address. What if she tracked me down and found out where I lived – and that I was actually a kitchen maid, not a journalist?

"I've got to go—"

"Fine." I realised I couldn't stop her. There was just one last thing I thought of to ask her. "Ethel? One last thing? Have you told the police about this woman?"

Ethel looked both truculent and scared. "I don't talk to the police," she said. "Not me." And with that, she opened the door, letting light and air into the dark, smoky saloon, and was gone.

I TOOK THE UNDERGROUND TRAIN home deep in thought. Obviously I was going to have to tell Inspector Marks about Ethel and what she'd seen at the rooming house. He'd virtually told me to 'report back' anything I might have discovered, and I wasn't going to let him down. It seemed obvious to me that this woman, whoever she was, was the key to this murder. But who was she? And why could the police find no trace of her? *Like a ghost.* I stared, unseeing, out of the dark windows of the train into the blackness of the tunnel wall beyond. Despite myself, I shivered.

I could feel that little niggle inside me that I'd felt once before, the itch and fidget of feeling that I was missing something, something important. What was it? It was something to do with the theatre, that was the only thing I could say for certain. The theatre was important in solving this case but how was it? And how could I work out its meaning and significance?

I was so lost in thought I almost missed my stop. Jumping up just as the guard blew his whistle in warning that he was about to shut the gate, I leapt off the train just before he crashed it shut. The clock on the platform wall was almost unreadable through the accumulation of grime on its glass face, but I squinted and could just see that it was almost five and twenty past nine. Time I was home before Mr Fenwick locked up for the night.

I walked a little nervously down the street. I wasn't used to being out on my own so late. At least this area, being well to do and respectable, was well-lit, and I could see the reassuring shape of a policeman up ahead on the corner, his cape swinging behind him as he patrolled the street. He gave me a nod as I went by and I smiled back politely.

I let myself into the basement by the kitchen door, expecting it to be in darkness. I knew Mrs Watling would have gone to her room as early as she could once everything had been left ready for tomorrow. I was surprised to see a light on in the scullery and even more surprised, once I got to the doorway, to see Verity bent over the stone sink in the corner of the room, the one we used for washing out the more heavily soiled saucepans and pots.

"What are you doing here?" I exclaimed. I had thought she would be out until late, waiting for Dorothy in the cloakroom as her mistress dined out at the Silk Club.

Verity looked up. I saw she was rinsing out one of her black dresses. She looked grim. "We had to come back early. Dorothy was sick on me."

I thought for a second I'd misheard her. "*Sick* on you? What? Is she ill?"

Verity half laughed. "Yes, she's suffering from a bad case of too many cocktails."

"Oh, Lord." I went over to see if I could help. "Seriously? She was sick on you? Where?"

Verity looked even grimmer. "In the back of the car. Andrew and I had to virtually *pour* her in. I suppose at least nobody saw, apart from us two."

I grimaced. "How horrible for you. What happened? Why did she get so – so inebriated?"

Verity gave her dress a last twist, releasing as much water as possible and then shook it out. It flapped damply. "I don't know. She's been drinking a lot more lately. It's been worrying me, to tell you the truth."

I remembered then, the smell of brandy I'd noticed when Dorothy and I had met to discuss the menu for Inspector Marks' visit. "I know she's not happy," I volunteered tentatively.

Verity sighed. She rolled her dress up and put it over on the counter. "I know. And I can't blame her exactly. It's just – I don't know what to do."

It occurred to me that our employers got a damn good deal out of us servants. Not only did we work like slaves for our money, we also became emotionally entangled with the job. I could see Verity was truly worried about her mistress.

I put an arm around her shoulders. "Try not to worry, V. It's not our place to judge, or – or have to worry about what to do. It's not up to us."

Verity sighed again. "Yes, I know. It's just – I hate seeing her do this to herself." She stopped talking for a moment and then said, with difficulty, "I don't know how much longer I can go on shielding her. Sooner or later someone's going to notice and then there's going to be a big scandal."

I didn't say anything for a moment. She was right. If Dorothy had been a man, she might have got away with it – for a while, at least. But while women of the upper classes were expected to drink, they were most definitely expected to be able to behave themselves while doing so.

"Perhaps we could ask someone for help?" I

suggested, knowing even as I spoke the words that there wasn't anyone. The thought of going to Mr Fenwick or Mrs Anstells and asking them for advice about what to do for our drunken mistress made me feel quite weak.

Verity pulled the plug from the sink and put it up on the side. The water ran down the pipes with a gurgle. "Come on, I'm just about all in. Let's go up."

We were walking towards the stairs when she remembered to ask me about my afternoon off. "How was it, Joanie? What did you do?"

I felt a leap of gladness that I now had someone to talk to. Perhaps it would take Verity's mind off things as well. "Well, it was very interesting, actually. Come on, I'll tell you all about it before we get to bed."

Chapter Thirteen

DOROTHY'S BREAKFAST TRAY CAME DOWN the next morning almost untouched. From what Verity had told me about the night before, I wasn't surprised. I wondered whether Dorothy would even make it out of bed that morning.

"Madam's hardly touched her tray," Mrs Watling commented. She looked worried, as if the uneaten food was a reflection of her cooking prowess.

"Don't worry, Mrs W, she's not very hungry this morning." Verity began to unload the untouched dishes onto the table. "I'll finish it off, I'm starving."

"Don't call me Mrs W," said Mrs Watling , but absently. Verity tipped me a wink across the table and began to polish off the uneaten bacon and eggs.

The morning's newspaper had come back down with the tray, also untouched, still neatly folded in thirds. As I carried the empty tray over to the dresser to wipe it down, I saw Verity flap open the newspaper to read the headlines. I had turned away by that point so I didn't see the expression on her face change but I *did* hear her suddenly choke.

I whirled around. "Verity? Are you all right?"

Verity was spluttering half-eaten bits of bacon over the table. "It's – my God! Look, Joan. It's Aldous! He's dead!" She broke into a thunderous fit of coughing that robbed her of further speech.

I felt as cold as if I'd suddenly been doused in ice-water. Hurrying over to the table, I grabbed the paper and saw for myself the glaring black headlines. ***Death of Young Actor. Body of Aldous Smith pulled from the Thames. Police believe it may be suicide.***

Horrified, I read on in increasing disbelief. I was dimly aware of Mrs Watling giving Verity a glass of water and then both women joined me and read over my shoulder.

"My God," I said in a whisper. "Aldous killed himself. Why? Why would he do such a wicked thing?"

"The police *think* he killed himself," Verity said hoarsely. She coughed again and went on. "They only found his body yesterday night. *God*, how awful. Tommy will be distraught."

Mrs Watling had her hand to her mouth. She'd never met Aldous but she'd heard us talk about him. "The poor young man. He must have been feeling desperate." Shaking her head, she moved away from the table to refill the kettle. "He was an actor, wasn't he? They're awfully sensitive, these acting types, aren't they? Take things to heart, they do. Their reviews and such."

I re-read the article, over and over, in near disbelief. I'd only met Aldous twice but having seen him on stage as well, it seemed just as unlikely as it had the first time I'd read the report. Could he really have killed himself? He had been a strange one. Morose and moody, and disinclined to talk to anyone. But then Verity had said – hadn't she? – that he hadn't been like that before. I read the last line in the article once more. *This is the second tragedy to strike at the heart of the Connault Theatre in the last six weeks. The murder of foreign national Guido Bonsignore, stabbed to death in his seat in the Gods on November 14th, remains unsolved with the police investigation ongoing.*

I thought back to how I'd felt last night, the unscratched itch of something being awry, something I wasn't yet able to comprehend. Was that it? Was that the connection? *The theatre was the key to this case.* I put the newspaper down and stared across the kitchen, unseeing. Had Aldous had something to do with the death of Guido Bonsignore? Was that why he'd committed suicide? *Had* he committed suicide? And how could he have had anything to do with the death of Guido Bonsignore when he'd been on the stage when it had happened?

Again, I felt it – the quicksilver flash of something, something important that I just couldn't understand. Frustrated, I screwed up my face and shook my head but it was gone. If I could just have five minutes to sit down and *think*. Just five minutes to puzzle it out...

"Come on, Joan. I'm very sorry about poor Mr Smith but the fact is that we've got luncheon for ten people to cook, and it's not going to cook itself." Mrs Watling pulled the newspaper off the table and folded it up briskly. I swallowed down my annoyance and tried to pull my mind back to my work. Fat chance of getting five minutes' peace around here.

Verity had disappeared somewhere. I wasn't able to go and find her. Mrs Watling had me make a start on the potatoes and I had a mound the size of a small house – or so it seemed – to peel. I plopped myself down at the kitchen table and set to with a vegetable peeler, feeling resentful.

I DIDN'T SEE VERITY FOR the rest of the morning. All the while I was chopping and baking and rinsing and scraping, my thoughts kept returning to Aldous. How old had he been? Twenty five? Younger? Poor man, to have such a bleak outlook on life that he had felt there was no option but to kill himself. But did he? I asked myself that as I stirred the soup, blinking against the steam as if it would reveal the answer to me as in some mystical potion. Had he *actually* killed himself? Was his death anything to do with the murder at the theatre? Or was it just sheer bad luck, an accident, even? Aldous walking home by the river, his foot slipping, falling with a splash into the cold black waters of the Thames, nobody around to hear his cries for help? Or perhaps a robbery; thugs with knives and coshes accosting him on the way home from the theatre, demanding money, pushing him into the river when they'd taken his money? Perhaps they hadn't meant to kill him, simply to make sure they got away.

I shook my head again. Now I really *was* being fanciful. I tried to put the thought of poor Aldous from my mind and keep my attention on what I was doing.

VERITY DIDN'T APPEAR AT LUNCHEON either. I was beginning to get a little worried about her when she suddenly popped into the kitchen at about two o'clock, with her hat and gloves in her hand and a purposeful look on her face. She went straight for Mrs Watling and drew her to one side. I strained my ears to hear what they were talking about but Verity was murmuring in too low a tone for me to be able to overhear.

After about five minutes of unintelligible conversation, Verity came over to me. I dried my hands off on the tea-towel and looked at her with eyebrows raised.

"Come on, get your coat and things," she said. "We're off out."

My eyebrows shot even higher. "What are you talking about?"

Verity clicked her tongue impatiently. "Just come on, Joan. I've cleared it with Mrs Watling and Mrs Anstells. We've got two hours."

"What—" I began, but Verity pulled a face like she was sucking a lemon and nodded frantically towards the hook where my coat hung.

"Just come *on*."

Giving in, I grabbed my coat, found my gloves and hat and hastily pinned it on. Was I supposed to talk to Mrs Watling myself? I began to walk over to where she was rolling out pastry on the floury surface of the kitchen table but she waved a whitened hand to me and said "Be back before five, Joan, that's a good girl. And do give poor Mr Tommy my sincere condolences."

"What is going on?" I hissed to Verity as we hurried up the basement stairs. It was a horrible day, cold and sleety and with a wind that tugged at our hats so that we were forced to keep them on with one hand as we made our way down the street.

"It's fine, it's all arranged," said Verity, hunting in her bag for her purse. "Dorothy agreed that I could go and see Tommy, after this tragedy with Aldous, and if Dorothy was fine with it, Mrs Anstells wasn't going to kick up a fuss."

"That was kind of her," I said, as we hurried down into the relative shelter of the Underground.

Verity snorted. "You know Dorothy. Desperate for the gossip." I turned to her, a little shocked and she looked a bit ashamed and added "Well, perhaps she really is sorry. I suppose she's not made of stone."

"What did you tell Mrs Watling?" I asked as we made our away onto the crowded platform. I could hear the distant hiss and screech of the train as it approached us through the tunnels.

"Just the facts. She's a good woman, she knew that Aldous was a friend of ours. Well, of mine. Well, of Tommy's." Verity had to shout above the noise of the approaching train as it clattered loudly into the station.

"Besides," said Verity, as we took our seats inside. "There's no possibility of Dorothy being able to eat anything like a normal dinner tonight, and I told Mrs Watling that too. So you shouldn't have too much to do when we get back."

I smiled despite myself. "Hungover badly, is she?"

Verity said nothing but rolled her eyes. I could see her gaze go to a man, on the opposite side of the carriage, who was reading that morning's paper. I looked over myself and re-read those horrible headlines.

"Poor Aldous," I murmured.

Verity gave me a look I couldn't quite decipher. "Maybe," she said.

I scarcely heard her over the noise of the train. "Where are we actually going? To the theatre?"

"No, to the pub next door. You know what actors are like. They're already holding an impromptu wake. Just an excuse to get drunk, if you ask me."

"Verity!"

Again, Verity looked a little ashamed of herself. "I know, I know, I'm not being reasonable."

"What's wrong?"

Verity looked grim. "Oh, everything. Dorothy being the next best thing to a dipsomaniac and Tommy being out of work now, and Aldous killing himself or perhaps not..." She trailed off, looking across the swaying carriage.

I patted her gloved hand. "Look, it'll be all right. Tommy's got his pantomime role coming up, hasn't he? So he won't be out of work for long. And as for Aldous—" I broke off, unsure of what I was going to say. "It's desperately sad, of course. I'm sure there's nothing much else we can do except what we're going to do now, go and give our support."

"Perhaps you're right." Verity, who had been sitting hunched forward, collapsed against the back of her seat with a sigh. Then she looked over at me with a quizzical smile. "Besides, Joanie, we've hardly had a chance to discuss the most important thing lately, have we? What about this murder?"

I looked down at my gloves. It was odd but in this case, with what I thought was Inspector Marks' blessing to at least make a few enquiries of my own, I felt as if my feeble attempts at investigation were getting nowhere. I didn't even have any theories as to why Guido Bonsignore had been killed - nothing apart from that odd niggle of doubt that even now reoccurred to me.

"I don't know," I said slowly. "There's nothing more to add than what I've already told you. There's just *something*—" I broke off in frustration, and then tried again. "It's something to do with the theatre, V. That's all I can say. I just know that the theatre has a part to play, an important part."

"What do you mean?"

I shook my head. "I can't put my finger on it. Every time I think I've got a grip on it, it just slips away like - like an eel."

Verity sat there looking at me, clearly waiting for me to say more. But as the minutes of silence lengthened, she gave me a glance that was half impatient, half sympathetic, and eventually turned her face away.

Chapter Fourteen

THE PUB NEXT TO THE theatre had seemed quite roomy the time we'd visited it before. It no longer seemed that way – probably because the better part of the entire cast and crew were currently packed into it, nursing drinks and, in most cases, shedding tears quite freely. I could see a few old men at the bar, who were clearly locals but not part of the theatre crowd, casting glances about them in some alarm.

Verity and I battled through the weeping throng until we reached Tommy, who sat at a table at the back, with Gwen, the wardrobe mistress at his side. He didn't look upset. He looked angry.

"Tommy, I'm so, so sorry," said Verity, casting herself into his arms. He gave her a hug and kissed her on the top of her bright hair but said nothing.

"I am too," I said and at least at that, Tommy looked up and gave me a brief smile.

Somehow, we managed to find a couple of chairs and pull them up to the tiny table. There was an earthenware jug of ale in the middle and a stack of cloudy glasses. Tommy poured us both a glass without comment.

Silence – as much of a silence as you could find in that noisy place – fell, as Verity and I sipped our drinks.

"The police came round earlier," Tommy said abruptly, staring at his half-empty glass. I could see the glimmer of red at the roots of his dyed black hair. He wouldn't need to re-dye it now for the part, now that the play was over. "They found a note in his lodgings. Not a long note, just a scrap of paper, really."

We all looked at one another.

"What did it say?" asked Verity, tentatively.

"Not a lot. Something like "I find it hard to believe I can carry on living." Something like that."

"Oh, Lord," I said without thinking. "Poor Aldous."

Tommy re-filled his glass from the jug. I could tell, by the glassiness of his eyes, that he'd had quite a lot of ale already. "I knew there was something on his mind, I *knew* it. I just wish he'd been able to confide in me. Perhaps I could have helped, I don't know. Done *something,* at least." He drained the glass in three gulps and slammed it back on the table, making us girls jump. "Why did he have to do a silly thing like that for? The *stupid* boy."

"I know what it was," announced Gwen. Her

eyelids were reddened, matching the hue of her round cheeks.

Tommy gave her a look of dislike. "Come on, he wouldn't have – have done what he did because of *that*."

"He might have. He was silly about her."

Verity and I were looking from one of them to the other. "Silly about who?" I asked.

Gwen looked triumphant. "Caroline, of course. He was head over heels in love with her. He would have done anything for her."

"No, he wouldn't, don't be stupid." Tommy sounded more irritable than I'd ever heard him. "He liked her, and Caroline was kind to him, that's all."

Gwen tossed her head. "You can think that if you want. I know what I saw, it was *obvious*."

Having observed Aldous' behaviour around Caroline Carpenter, I could only agree with Gwen. Would that have been enough for Aldous to have killed himself, though? Did unrequited love hurt that much?

Silence fell again. Tommy refilled his glass yet again and drank moodily. I cast around for something to say, anything really, but couldn't think of anything that would sound suitable. After a moment, Verity drew her chair nearer Tommy's and took his hand. He turned to her and put his head on her shoulder.

For some reason, the gesture brought tears to

my eyes. He was like a little boy, all of a sudden. Feeling as if I were intruding on a private grief, I turned to Gwen.

"It must have been such a shock to you all," I said, nervously turning my glass around and around in my fingers.

"Oh, it was, it was." Gwen's normally cheerful face was troubled. "We all could scarcely believe it. Caroline just collapsed. She actually fainted."

I looked around the room, searching for Caroline, but couldn't see her. "Was she all right? Is she here?"

Gwen shook her head. "She's at her fiancé's house. I can't imagine she'll be back here anytime soon. I mean, what is there to come back to? The play's finished, Aldous is—" She broke off, fiddling with the sleeve of her blouse. Then she looked up directly into my eyes. "I should have told him not to waste his time mooning over *her*. She was never going to give up her rich, important fiancé for a struggling *actor*."

It occurred to me then that Gwen had been a little in love with Aldous Smith herself. I suppose that was understandable.

Gwen was still speaking, still with that undertone of bitterness in her voice. "Caroline loved him dancing attendance on her but she was just using him, that was all. Some people have all the luck, don't they? She's got it all, talent, beauty, all the men wanting her, and now riches and a place in society." Envy had thickened her voice so much that it was hard to make out what she was saying.

I felt helpless. What could I say against life's truth – that some people have it all, and others, like Gwen and me, have very little? Life wasn't fair. That was what it came down to, really. Life just wasn't fair.

As I had before, I tried to think of something to distract Gwen, something that would cheer her up. She'd obviously loved talking about her work before so I asked her about that.

"Had any more costume mishaps lately?" I enquired, rather desperately.

Gwen was still staring moodily at the tabletop, her fingers twisting the button of her cuff. She'd have that off if she wasn't careful. Mind you, if anyone could mend clothes, you'd think a wardrobe mistress would be able to. "What's that?"

"Anything funny happened lately with your costumes?"

For a moment I thought she wasn't going to answer me and then she seemed to sigh and bring herself back to reality. "Actually, it's funny you saying that. Something did happen the other day, I'd quite forgotten about it."

"What was that?"

"Oh, you know I said a costume had been stolen?" I couldn't remember that she'd said that but I nodded encouragingly. Gwen half laughed. "My eyes must have been playing tricks on me because I did actually find it again, stuffed into one of the back cupboards. Silly of me."

"Oh, well, that's a relief," I said, not really caring either way but glad that she seemed a little more cheerful.

Tommy and Verity had finished their whispered conversation. Tommy turned back to the table and tipped the last dregs of the jug into his glass. He'd put a small red book onto the table and I leant forward a little to see what it was. He saw me looking.

"The play. *Voyage of the Heart*."

"Oh." I leant forward even more. I'd never actually read a play in its original form before. "May I? I mean, could I have a look?"

Tommy tossed the book over to me. "Have it. It's of no use to me anymore. I may as well throw it in the bin."

"Oh, don't do that," I said, shocked. "May I really have it?"

The bleak tone in his voice lifted just a little. "Yes, Joan. Seriously, please keep it. Give it a good home."

"Well, thank you." I put it safely away in my bag. Something to read tonight, if I had the time and energy. I'd be able to see how a play should actually be set out on the page. It came to me then, what a wonderful thing it would be to write a play – an actual play. It was an arresting thought, and for a moment, I was lost in a dream of the future, of myself being a famous playwright, the best actors and actresses of the time bringing my characters to life.

I was so lost in a dream world that it took Verity several attempts to attract my attention. "Joan. Joan. It's nearly time to go. Come on, drink up."

"Sorry," I said, flustered.

Tommy leant his head back against the wall with a sigh. "The funeral is next week, apparently."

Verity squeezed his arm. "Would you like us to come? If we can get the time off, I mean?"

"That would be kind. But don't get into trouble on our account."

"We'll try. To come, I mean, not get into trouble," I said, feeling a bit ridiculous.

He smiled at me sadly. "Thank you, Joan."

There was another short silence and I was just about to get to my feet when Tommy remarked again. "I see Caroline's set the wedding date at last."

"Oh yes?" Verity said, beginning to pull on her gloves.

"Yes." Tommy shut his eyes as if exhausted. "In about three weeks' time, she'll no longer be Caroline Carpenter but Mrs Nicolas Holmes. Wife of an MP, God help her."

"Well, she should be used to the name change,

at least," said Gwen, with a touch of vinegar in her voice.

"What do you mean?" Verity asked, just before I got the chance.

"Oh, Caroline Carpenter's her stage name. Goodness knows what her real name was. Edna Grubb, or something, probably."

Verity and I smiled, despite ourselves. Then, because time was ticking along, we kissed Tommy, bid Gwen goodbye, and began the struggle through the crowded pub towards the exit.

Chapter Fifteen

As it happened, Verity was able to attend the funeral but I wasn't. Mrs Watling, kind as she had been to let me go and give my condolences to Tommy that night at the pub, flatly refused to allow me to attend the funeral of a man I'd barely known. I couldn't really blame her. As it was, I gave Verity a kiss goodbye on the morning of the funeral and then went back to work, trying not to mind too much.

It was baking day, as it was every Tuesday. I pounded the bread dough with my fists, working out some of my frustration. That was the problem with being a servant – well, I suppose it was like that with any job, really. It wasn't the money, it was the fact that your time wasn't your own. After the dough was placed in the bottom oven of the range to proof and rise, I turned my attention to the biscuits and scones that were next on the list, wondering about the funeral and how Verity and Tommy would be feeling. Would Caroline be there? Of course she would, I chastised myself.

Once everything was either in the oven or turned out onto the wire rack to cool, I had a precious half hour in which to sit down, have a cup of tea, and think. Or, if not think, read the play that Tommy had given me the previous week. I turned the book over in my hands, thinking how odd it was that the words contained within it could engender such passion and emotion when acted on stage. I'd never actually sat down and *read* a play, in its original state, before. I opened the covers a little nervously.

It was more difficult than I'd expected, to be honest. I was so used to reading things in novels and newspapers that the lay-out of the words on the page in the play put me off a bit. I struggled through the first few pages, wondering if I could be bothered to continue. But then, I recognised a bit of dialogue – I could remember Caroline Carpenter saying it, on stage – and then the play sprang to life for me and after that it was easy. I was engrossed.

Half an hour slips by quickly when you're doing something you actually want to do. Before I knew it, the clock was pointing to twelve o'clock and I had to heave myself out of the chair, put the play to one side, and return to work.

The afternoon slipped by and I was busy enough not to worry too much about the funeral and how Tommy and Verity must be feeling. I'd just put the finishing touches to Dorothy's main course – a rack of lamb with redcurrant jelly, chipped potatoes, and three vegetable dishes to accompany it – when the back door to the kitchen opened, letting in a rush of wintry air.

It was Verity, returned from the funeral. One look at her was enough to make me realise quite how much of a toll it had taken from her.

"Are you all right?"

Verity shook her head. I could tell she was near tears, and that, in itself, was alarming. Verity almost never cried, unlike me, who could weep at the drop of a hat.

"Was it very bad?"

"It's not just that," Verity said wearily. She pulled her gloves off, pulled the hatpins from her hair, and then threw her hat into a corner of the room with a viciousness that startled me.

"Verity—"

"I don't want to talk about it, Joan. Not just yet. Besides, I have to get back to Dorothy."

Mrs Watling, who'd been down at the markets, came in through the back door with her hands piled with brown-paper-wrapped packages. "Oh, Verity, you're back," she exclaimed and then took a look at Verity's face. "Oh – oh, dear. Was it so very bad?"

I braced myself but Verity didn't say anything. She sort of slumped out of the room, without even stopping to pick up her discarded hat. Mrs Watling tutted and bent down to retrieve it, dusting it off.

"I'm sorry," I said, although why I was apologising I didn't know.

Mrs Watling put the hat on the dresser, out of the way. "Funerals are terribly hard," she said, without anger. "Particularly when it's a young one. Such a terrible waste."

Verity's return and the bad mood she brought with her cast a pall over the evening. Mrs Watling, Doris and I served up the dinner for the servants, washed up the dishes and tidied the kitchen, preparing it as usual for tomorrow, but we didn't talk much as we were doing it, and Doris didn't do her usual trick of singing the popular music hall hits in her off-key warble. I think the only words we said to one another after nine o'clock were 'goodnight'.

I climbed the stairs on weary legs, *Voyage of the Heart* in my hand. I wanted to read some more before I went to sleep, but I felt so tired I wasn't sure I was going to be able to stay awake. For some reason, I had expected Verity to be with Dorothy still, so I jumped when I walked into our room and found her curled up on the bed.

"Oh, V..." As I got closer, I could see she had been crying, although she was dry-eyed now. I wanted to give her something to make her feel better – what, I wasn't sure of. A chocolate bar, a sweet, a drink –

just something. But I had nothing to give. I patted her on the back instead.

She rolled over onto her back and gave me a wan smile. "Sorry, Joanie. I was very snappy and horrible to you earlier."

"No, you weren't."

"I was."

"Well, anyway. It doesn't matter. It's been a hard day."

Verity briefly closed her eyes. "Oh, Joan, you have no idea. It was *horrible*. Aldous's parents were there, *distraught,* of course, and the vicar kept skirting around the fact that he'd killed himself, like it was this big, shameful secret – which I suppose it is – and everyone was there, thinking about it but not being able to say anything or talk about it or anything—" she stopped and swallowed, as if it hurt her. "And Caroline turned up with her fiancé, looking like a fashion plate and brought all the newspaper men with her and sobbed like it was going out of fashion..."

I waited for her to say more but she didn't. "The press were there?"

"Of course they were. It's got it all, hasn't it? Scandalous suicide of handsome young actor, involvement of beautiful famous young actress who's about to marry that stuffed shirt MP. Tie in the murder at the Connault. Sprinkle in a few more semi-famous names. It's the story that's got it all."

She rubbed her face hard and let her hands drop back down to her side. "I hope Tommy's going to be all right. He was three sheets to the wind before the funeral even started."

"Oh, dear." It was a most inadequate remark but what else could I say? "How's Dorothy this evening?" I asked, cautiously.

Verity heaved herself off the bed with a groan. "Quiet, thank God. Subdued. Just as well, I don't think I could have taken any more drama." She went over to the dressing table and sat down to begin unpinning her hair.

I started to get undressed, my thoughts far away. For a moment, I almost forgot Verity was in the room. Then I was startled by her asking me a question.

"What's that?"

Verity had stopped unpinning her hair. She was staring at her reflection in the mirror as if mesmerised by it. "I said, don't you ever wonder – don't you ever worry that this is it?"

"What do you mean, this is it?"

"I mean, this is *it*. For your life. This is all that's ever going to happen. That you're just going to be a servant for the rest of your life, until you die."

Her melancholy tone worried me. I don't think I'd ever heard her speak in quite such a way before. "Well, I suppose I do. Sometimes. But—"

"But what?"

I sat down on the bed, catching her gaze in the reflection of the mirror. "Well, I – I've got ambition. I don't want to be a servant for the rest of my life."

"Nor do I," said Verity, with emphasis. "But what else can we do? Get married?"

"Do you want to?" It seemed funny then, that neither Verity nor I had ever really talked about getting married.

Verity snorted. "It wouldn't matter if I wanted to or not. When do we ever meet anyone anyway? Any men? There's no bloody *time* to meet anyone, whether I wanted to marry them or not."

"Well—" I had to pause. She was right of course. Apart from our evenings out, we had no time to meet any men, suitable or otherwise. And the men in the household were either ancient or not interested – at least not interested in someone like me. I thought, with a touch of bitterness, that at least Verity had prettiness and vivacity on her side. What did I have, except for a few cooking skills? You've got nice hair, I told myself, in a desperate attempt to find something positive to say about myself. But what man ever fell for someone who just had nice hair – and no other alluring attributes?

I had always assumed I would get married and have children one day, because that was just what you did, if you were a girl. I tried to think of someone of my class who wasn't married, and did something else instead. I discounted people like

Dorothy. When you're wealthy, you can do as you want. But was there anyone I knew, in my social sphere, who wasn't married and yet did something that was interesting?

"What about Gwen?" I said, hearing the doubt in my voice even as I mentioned her name. "She's got a career, hasn't she? And she's not married."

That was a pathetic example, even I could see that. You could tell that Gwen, nice as she was, was in no small way terribly bitter about being single. You just had to listen to her little digs at Caroline to see that.

Verity snorted again but didn't bother to respond. She yanked the few remaining pins out of her hair with bad grace. "I feel like swearing, really swearing," she said, after a moment's silence.

"Well, what's stopped you before?" I asked.

"No, I mean, *really* swearing. Those actors are a bad influence."

"Well, don't really swear. You won't feel any better for doing so."

"Maybe." I could see her staring moodily at her reflection again.

In an effort to get her mind off the subject, I fastened on the closest thing to hand. "I've been reading Tommy's play, you know, *Voyage of the Heart*. It's wonderful."

"Oh yes?" I could tell Verity wasn't really listening to me.

"That's it," I said, somewhat desperately. "That's what we'll do. We won't bother getting married. I'll write plays and you can act in them. I always said you'd be a wonderful actress."

There was a short, loaded silence. Verity's eyes came round to meet mine in the mirror.

"What a wonderful idea," she said, slowly.

Of course, the second I'd made it, I started backpedalling immediately. "Well, it sounds good, I'll grant you but—"

"You'd be a brilliant playwright. I've read your stories, they're marvellous."

"But – but—"

"But, what? Joanie, it's a marvellous idea."

"But – I don't know how to write plays." I'd forgotten that I'd vowed just a few days ago that I was going to look into how I would go about writing professionally.

Verity thrust her hands into her hair and shook it out, a fountain of red-gold over her shoulders. She turned to me, her eyes sparkling, her dark mood of just moments before obviously gone. "Joanie, I always said you're a genius. What a marvellous idea. You can write the plays, we'll take them to Tommy and he can find a director and then I'll act in them." She got up and then cast herself upon her bed, giggling. "We'll both be famous. Just think of it!"

I started to laugh too. This was the Verity I knew,

impulsive and spontaneous and full of enthusiasm for the future. "Oh yes. It'll be easy as pie, I'm sure."

"Well, what have we got to lose?"

I laughed harder. "Our jobs?"

Verity's giggles died away. "Oh well, yes, I suppose so." She sat up, the inner light inside her suddenly quenched. "I suppose you're right."

I couldn't bear to see her cast down again. "It's not a stupid idea, V. It's just – you took me by surprise, that's all."

We stared at each other. I think we both knew the conversation wasn't finished but the exhaustion that we'd both been fending off suddenly hit us. Verity dropped her gaze, yawning. "I'm all in, Joan. Let's sleep. We'll talk about it in the morning."

"All right," I agreed. I got up off the bed to continue undressing. "It's been a strange day, V. Let's not make any hasty decisions right now."

"No, you're right."

I pulled on my nightdress. I had that unsatisfactory feeling of a conversation cut short, of a discussion that we should have been having suddenly cut off. After a moment, I picked up my washbag. "You can turn off the light, if you want," I said. "I'll be quiet when I come back in."

"Very well, Joanie. Good night."

"Good night."

Verity got into bed with a sigh and switched off the lamp. In the blackness that followed, I stood for a moment, temporarily blinded. In my head was the swish of the red velvet curtains of the stage and the roar of applause from the crowd sitting in the darkness beyond the footlights.

Chapter Sixteen

OF COURSE, VERITY AND I didn't get a chance to talk at all the next morning. Dorothy was off for a luncheon date with some of her girl chums and Verity had to go with her. We barely had time to give each other a nod before she was out the front door, and I had no idea when she'd be back.

Things had been so fraught and busy I'd almost forgotten about my conversation with Ethel, the girl at the rooming house of Guido Bonsignore. That was something I *had* to tell Inspector Marks. But how on Earth was I supposed to go and see him when my next afternoon off wasn't for three days? I'd taxed Mrs Watling's patience to the limit with our impromptu trip to see Tommy, the week before, and there was no possible way for me to get to Scotland Yard without seriously endangering my position.

It made me snappy and irritable. Poor Doris got the rough end of my tongue more than once, and I could sense Mrs Watling giving me nervous, sideways looks as we prepared luncheon for the servants. As was usual, I made an effort to bite down on my bad temper, but even so, I had to walk into the larder a few times to bury my face in a teatowel and scream out my anger and frustration in a choked-off sort of way.

After lunch, I grew calmer. I'd been thinking about what I had to do and once I'd decided, it made all my histrionics and bad temper seem rather foolish. Before I could prevaricate, I found Inspector Marks' card, walked to Mr Fenwick's telephone, and calmly dialled the number.

There was a bit of a kerfuffle before I actually managed to get through to the inspector himself, and by then, my temporary confidence had deserted me. When his familiar voice spoke down the line, I had to stop myself from stammering and stuttering in relief.

"It's Joan – Joan Hart. Inspector. Sorry."

"Miss Hart. How are you?"

I stuttered out something about being fine. "I – I—"

The inspector's voice was warm and kind and I felt myself begin to relax as he spoke. "Do you have something to tell me?"

"Yes. Yes, I do, but I'm afraid I can't get out – I mean, I don't have any more time off so I can't come and see you—"

I was becoming incoherent again. Thankfully, I

heard him say, "That's quite all right, Miss Hart. I know what's it's like for you working girls. I'll come to you. Are you free this evening?"

"No," I said in confusion. "Not really. I mean I have to—"

"I'm sorry, I meant, will you get into trouble if I call around to see you this evening? About nine o'clock?"

"Oh." I could feel the heat in my cheeks. "No, that would be fine. I'll tell Mrs Watling I'm expecting you." That made me blush even harder.

"Very well. I'll look forward to seeing you then."

"Goodbye," I said, scarcely able to talk, and put the telephone receiver back in its cradle. I walked back to the kitchen as if I were in a dream.

Somehow I got through the rest of the afternoon. Dorothy only wanted a simple supper that evening, which helped. Pea and ham soup, which was nice and easy, lamb chops with accompaniments and a simple fruit flan for dessert. Mrs Watling and I made a stew for the servants and there was enough of the soup for us all to have a bowl of that as well.

Although it had been a fairly calm afternoon, there was still enough to do to keep me from thinking about what Verity and I had discussed last night. In the cold reality of day, it seemed even more fantastical. Surely I, a lowly servant girl, wouldn't be able to write a play? Much less have it performed by real actors? I helped Doris clear the dinner table and carried the dirty plates into the scullery for her to wash, working mechanically, not really thinking of the task in hand. Could I do it? Where would I start? What would I write about? And when on Earth was I ever going to get the *time*?

By the evening, I was mentally exhausted from the thoughts fireworking around and around in my head – not to mention my growing anxiety about my upcoming meeting with Inspector Marks. I told myself that I really did have something important to tell him, and I wasn't making the poor man come all the way across town on a wild goose chase. By the time it got to half an hour before he was expected, I realised I hadn't even mentioned that he was arriving to Mrs Watling.

"Oh – um, Mrs Watling? Inspector Marks will be popping in this evening, about nine. He wants to talk to us." I had no idea why I'd just said 'us' instead of me. Perhaps because it sounded a little less embarrassing.

"Inspector Marks? What on Earth does he want to talk to us about?" Mrs Watling, who'd been sitting dozing off in her armchair by the range, snapped awake again. When I saw how much of a panic she was in, I felt bad that I hadn't mentioned it before. I should have broken the news a little more gently.

"Please don't worry. I think it's me he wants to talk to anyway. It's probably to do with the theatre case."

Mrs Watling had a fluttering hand to her chest, as if to calm her racing heartbeat. "I'm sure I don't know why the police have to keep bothering us. You'd hope that would all be finished with at long last, now his Lordship's case is over." Her hand stilled a little and she gave me a sideways glance that was at once suspicious and curious. "Hold on a minute, Joan. The Inspector's coming to see *you*?"

Something in the way she said it made me shuffle my feet. "Well, yes, I suppose so."

"Is he married?"

I knew exactly what she was trying to imply and tried to laugh it off, ignoring the rising heat in my face which I knew she would have seen. "He just needs to talk to me about the case, that's all. Nothing more."

"That's not what I asked. Is he married?"

"I don't know," I answered honestly. "But—"

"It's just that you're so young, Joan. Don't have your head turned by a man, even if he is a police inspector. You've no female relatives, and I feel it's my duty to keep an eye on you, to make sure you don't find yourself in any trouble."

The unworthy thought popped into my head that Mrs Watling just didn't want to lose her hard worker to marriage. Not that I had any expectations in the direction at all, but... I tried to smile and look unbothered and I said, as firmly as I could, "Mrs Watling, I'm sure the inspector is here purely and simply in a professional capacity, that's all."

As if on cue, I heard the doorbell upstairs go, and despite my efforts to remain calm and unflustered, I jumped a little, saw to my annoyance that Mrs Watling had noticed and turned sharply away to refill the kettle, mostly to have something to do with my hands.

I could hear Mr Fenwick's footsteps overhead and then a double set of footsteps approaching the door to the basement at the end of the hallway.

"I'll be in my parlour," Mrs Watling said, heaving herself to her feet as the footsteps approached closer. "With the door open," she added in a dark tone.

As soon as I set eyes on Inspector Marks, my nervousness vanished. Partly it was the kind smile that I received, partly it was something inside me that just settled, as if I'd been rushing around in circles for hours and then all of a sudden, peace and calm descended. I did have one moment of hesitation, where I wasn't sure whether to shake hands or not, and covered my confusion with reaching for the full teapot.

"Now, Joan," said the inspector. "I've only got a bare half hour, I'm afraid."

"That's quite understandable, sir. I'm very grateful that you've come here to save me a journey. Very grateful indeed." I handed him a steaming cup of tea, hesitated, and then added, "I'm sure you must be wanting to get back to your family."

The inspector smiled rather sadly. "I'm afraid I

don't have one, Joan. Not one of my own. My wife died several years ago."

"Oh, I'm sorry," I exclaimed. "Oh, I'm so very sorry, sir. That must have been terribly hard for you."

"It was." He sipped his tea briefly and I got the impression he didn't want to talk about it anymore, so I sat down myself opposite him and picked up my own teacup. Then, because I just couldn't leave it at that, I said impulsively, "I know what it's like to be all alone in the world, sir. I grew up in an orphanage."

"I'm sorry to hear that." Our eyes met through the rising steam from the cups and I felt again that flash of warmth as we silently understood one another.

"Besides," I added, in the interest of fairness. "I've got my good friend Verity, Miss Hunter. So I'm not all alone, exactly."

"A good friend is a valuable thing," agreed Inspector Marks. Then I could see him setting sentiment aside. "Now, Miss Hart – Joan? What did you have to tell me?"

I didn't prevaricate but came straight to the point. I wanted to match his professionalism and his no-nonsense air of getting things done.

"There's a girl called Ethel who works at the rooming house where Guido Bonsignore lived. I spoke to her a few days ago, and she told me she'd seen a woman visit Guido a week or so before he died." I went on to recount, as meticulously as possible, Ethel's and my conversation. I wavered for a moment as to whether to confess I'd pretended to be a journalist but I was pretty sure that wasn't a criminal offence and – I'll be honest – I wanted to impress Inspector Marks, so I was honest about it. He said nothing but I saw him smile.

"Well, I must say you have quite a knack at finding new witnesses, Joan," was all that he said once he'd scribbled down everything that I'd said in his little notebook. "I'm not sure how my men missed her on our first investigations at the house."

"Well, sir, she said she wouldn't talk to the police. And she's a servant. We're pretty much invisible to everybody," I added, with a touch of bitterness.

"Well, thank you, Joan. I think I might be able to persuade Miss Ethel to talk to us after all. Is there anything else?"

"Actually, I have a question for you, if that's not too impertinent, sir?"

He looked at me curiously. "What is it, Joan?"

I took a deep breath. "Sir, I'm sure I remember you telling me before that you thought Guido Bonsignore was actually a false name."

"Yes, that's right. It was."

I hesitated again. It wasn't really any of my business, was it? But I really wanted to know... "Do you – do you know what his real name was?"

The inspector regarded me for a moment, rubbing one finger across his black moustache. For a second, I thought he was going to say just that, that it wasn't any of my business and then he nodded. "His real name was Gideon Bonnacker."

I mouthed the words silently and then said them aloud. "'Gideon Bonnacker." For a moment I felt a little jab of disappointment. Had I expected that the second I heard the real name of the murder victim, that I'd be able to solve the case there and then? The name meant nothing to me. Literally nothing.

The inspector was still watching me. He leaned forward a little. "He was travelling on a false passport. You'd be surprised how easy they are to get hold of, particularly after the war. There was all sorts of black market trade in different identification papers from people killed in the conflict. There still is."

"Yes, I see." I turned my teacup around in my hands, thinking. "Why would he come back under a false name? Was there an arrest warrant out for him, under his real name, I mean?"

The inspector looked pleased. "Now you're thinking like a detective, Joan. It's a good question, but as a matter of fact, there wasn't. He'd grown up in England, fought and survived the war, went back out to Europe about twelve years ago, and he's lived in Italy ever since. Had lived, I should say."

"So he led a blameless life, sir?"

The inspector's smile dimmed. "I'm not so sure about that, Joan. People who truly do lead blameless lives don't tend to find themselves stabbed to death in theatres. But yes, so far as we can ascertain, there's nothing particularly striking in Gideon Bonnacker's life, unlike his death. He left his last place of employment in Italy under something of a cloud, it seems, but there were no criminal charges brought. He was sailing pretty close to the wind financially, although his bank account does show some reasonably large cash sums deposited over the last few months. The landlady of his rooming house told my men that there was a pretty regular Friday night poker game that took place there, so it might be that he won it over the cards."

"I see," I said again. Then, thinking of something else, added, "He was a bit of a gambler, then?"

"So it seems. I've had positive identification of him at several of the race tracks. Rather bizarrely, it seemed he was also a regular at the local Catholic Church."

I nodded. Both of those were worlds I knew absolutely nothing about and again, I felt a surge of disappointment, almost of frustration, that I wasn't being of any more help whatsoever. I did have one other question, though and I hoped I wasn't pushing my luck by asking the inspector.

"Sir, this might sound strange but did the doctors – did they manage to pinpoint the time of

Guido, I mean, Gideon's death more accurately? You said you were waiting for the post-mortem last time we spoke about it."

The inspector stared at me, curiously. Then obviously deciding to humour me, he nodded and said "It seems likely that he was killed within the first half hour of the play. It's not set in stone, but the doctors thought that they could narrow it down that far, at least."

I thought back to that night, remembered pressing my fingers against the veins and arteries in his neck. "Yes, that does make sense. When I took his pulse, he was cool. Not cold, but the warmth had gone completely."

The inspector courteously waited for me to go on but I had nothing else to say on the subject. He sat up briskly. "Well, if that's everything?" He drained his teacup, wiped his moustache with his pocket handkerchief and made as if to stand up. I got up quickly myself, wondering if there was anything else I could say – or ask. *I hope you've been listening*, I thought to myself, sending a rather dour message to Mrs Watling in the privacy of my own head. *No dalliances here. Worst luck.*

"Well, Joan, you've got my card, so don't hesitate to call if there's anything else you remember, or that you think we might need to hear. I appreciate your help."

He smiled at me, kind as always. I tried to smile

back, conscious that there would be no reason for me to telephone him again. What else could I tell him? I'd tried to do a bit of investigation and that had all really come to nothing, hadn't it? I felt again that keen sense of ridiculousness, that I, Joan Hart, really thought I'd do better than the police and trained professionals. Who did I think I was?

The inspector shook my hand. I had a sudden, horrid, paranoid thought then – that Inspector Marks was encouraging me to do my own detective work so that he could have a good laugh at me and my delusions of grandeur. Was he setting me up for a giant fall? Surely not? He wouldn't be that unkind, would he? Of course he wouldn't, I told myself, but that treacherous little voice refused to stay quiet. I was irresistibly reminded of that quotation from Samuel Johnson, about the walking dog. *Sir, a woman's preaching is like a dog's walking on his hind legs. It is not done well; but you are surprised to find it done at all.* Replace 'preaching' with 'investigation' – was that how Inspector Marks thought of me?

I was feeling so miserable that I scarcely managed a goodbye smile. I managed to raise a hand to wave to him as he walked from the kitchen, heading for the front door. Then I slumped back down at the kitchen table and put my head in my hands, feeling like a failure at everything.

Chapter Seventeen

MY LOW MOOD PERSISTED FOR much of the week. I didn't pick up *Voyage of the Heart* again, not even late at night to read in bed. It remained on my beside table, reproaching me for my weak will and laziness every time I looked at it. I scarcely had the energy to glance through the newspaper every day, although I did give it a cursory skim every morning, just to see if there was anything else about the Connault murder. But day after day, there was nothing, not even the realisation that the victim had at least been positively identified. There was a short article about the funeral of Aldous Smith, which I read eagerly, but there was little substance to it, just a series of photographs, mostly of Caroline Carpenter looking extremely glamourous, even with a little black nose veil shielding her face.

I put the newspaper down on the table, staring at the photograph. Something about that was ringing a bell. What was it? After a moment, it came to me. Ethel had mentioned the woman coming to see Guido – or Gideon Bonnacker – and the fact that she'd had a black veil on covering her face. I looked again at the black and white newsprint, the reproduction of Caroline's lovely face. Was it so ridiculous to think that it might have been *Caroline* who had called to see Gideon?

That thought lasted half a minute – perhaps not even that – before I realised I was being *completely* ridiculous. Why would Caroline go and visit a perfect stranger in a seedy rooming house? And how could she have been the woman in the Gods on the night of the murder when she'd actually been *on stage* in the very first act of the play? I snorted to myself. Some detective I'd make. Where was the motive? Come to that, where was the opportunity? And without those two things, where was the evidence?

I dismissed the thought entirely from my head, closed the newspaper, and made a resolution: I was going to forget about this whole case. It was clearly having a deleterious effect on my mind and my mood. All my investigations – such pathetic ones as they had been – were doing nothing to help and they were making me actively unhappy. I made another resolution, that'd I'd start to re-read *Voyage of the Heart* tonight, if I wasn't too tired by the time I got to bed, and I'd make a real effort to start thinking about writing my own play – even if I wasn't at all sure how to go about it.

I made a concerted effort to get on top of all my

chores that afternoon. As was usual, once I'd stopped moaning to myself and sulking about feeling martyred, the day flew by in a much more cheerful manner, and Mrs Watling actually complimented me on the rack of lamb that I produced for Dorothy that evening, though she was dining alone. After tidying up the kitchen and making sure everything was ready for tomorrow, I carried a tea tray up to the bedroom, so I could enjoy a cuppa whilst reading the play. I thought I might even make a start at mapping out some of the plot and characters of my own play.

Verity came in at about ten o'clock, slightly flushed and more giggly than was normal for her.

"What's wrong with you?" I eyed her over the rim of my mug. "Have you been drinking?"

"Yes, actually." Verity flopped down onto her bed and rubbed her eyes. "Dorothy wanted me to dine with her, and I had to have two glasses of wine, otherwise she would have drunk up the whole bottle. That's the second bottle tonight."

"What?"

Verity rolled her eyes. "She'd put away a whole bottle by the time dinner arrived. So I had to have a couple of glasses from the other one, otherwise she'd have been face down in your lovely dinner before too long."

I gave her a wry look. "What a noble sacrifice you made."

Verity giggled harder. "There are some perks to being a lady's maid, you know."

"Don't I know it! The food was acceptable, then? Mrs Watling was pleased with me for the main dish."

"It was lovely. Oof, I'm so full of food and wine I might burst." She sat down to unbuckle her shoes and looked up at me slightly tipsily. "Anyway, what about you? You could have done with a bit of a pick-me-up yourself, you know, Joan. You've been a right misery all week."

"I know," I admitted. "But I'm over it now."

"What was wrong?"

"Oh, nothing. Nothing and everything."

Verity gave me a sympathetic looks. "Were you so very upset about Aldous?"

Honesty made me dissuade her that that had been the problem. "No, it wasn't that. It was just – perhaps I was trying to make sense of it all. I wasn't getting very far."

Verity nodded and pulled her dress over her head, dropping it on the floor a second later. "Whoops. Anyway, there's no need to be melancholy. Tommy's pantomime run starts next week, and if I'm not very much mistaken, he'll be sending us tickets for when they do the dress rehearsal."

This did indeed cheer me up further. We'd been to several of these dress rehearsal performances, where the tickets were so cheap (or, lucky us, free) that nobody minded so much if somebody forgot their lines, or doors were opened wrongly on the stage or props got dropped or missed completely. It was all part of the fun and, as a lot of the audience at those shows was made up of friends and family of the crew, there was sometimes quite a lively party afterwards.

"Oh, good." By now I was yawning over the play, despite the tea, and decided to leave it for the next night. Perhaps I would dream up a plot in my sleep, who knew? There was one thing I checked just before I put the book to one side and turned out the bedside light. Curious, I checked the first act, just to see if I'd remembered correctly. Yes, I had; Caroline's character had been on stage for almost all of the first act, certainly for the first four scenes which meant there was no possible way the woman in the Gods had been her. But it wouldn't have been her anyway, would it? What on Earth had it to do with her? I must have been mad, thinking like that, and it was a sign that I should probably leave well enough alone.

Verity came back from the bathroom and stumbled into the edge of her bed as she divested herself of her slippers. "Whoops."

I giggled despite myself. "Go to sleep, you drunkard. See you in the morning."

"Goo' night."

I chuckled to myself as I turned over in my bed, pulling the covers up to my chin.

VERITY HAD A BIT OF a headache the next morning, unsurprisingly, but that was nothing to how Dorothy was obviously feeling. Again, her breakfast tray came down almost untouched, apart from the coffee pot which had been drained dry. I saw Mrs Watling looking it over and frowning and when Verity came back downstairs a half an hour or so later for more coffee, she beckoned her over.

"Is her ladyship ill, Verity? She doesn't seem to have touched her breakfast, and that's the third or fourth time she's eaten hardly anything."

"Oh, she's just feeling a bit under the weather," Verity said. Her gaze caught mine for a moment and I found myself making a rueful face, which unfortunately Mrs Watling saw.

"What is it, Joan?"

"Nothing, nothing," I said hurriedly. I turned back to the dough I was making, hearing Verity tell Mrs Watling some goodnatured lie about Dorothy having trouble shaking off a cold.

"I'll make her up some rosehip tea," said Mrs Watling. "There's nothing better if you're coming down with a cold."

"Wonderful," said Verity. She shot me a neutral gaze, which nevertheless said everything that she intended it to, picked up the refilled coffee pot and left the room.

I got on with my work, thinking about our

mistress. Was there anything we could do? I didn't think there was. It was most decidedly not our place to advise our employer that she was drinking far too much. I wondered if Mr Fenwick had noticed how much wine Dorothy was getting through, seeing as he was the one responsible for ordering and decanting it. There wasn't any way to ask him, either. It's not your place to worry about it, I told myself, thumping the dough. I seemed to be saying that to myself a lot lately.

Dorothy must have got over her hangover because she dined out that night and took Verity with her as a companion. Early on in her role, I had mentioned to Verity how nice it must be to get to go out to dinner at posh places, and jazz clubs, and exciting restaurants, and she'd rolled her eyes. "Most of the time I have to wait for her in the cloakroom, Joan," she said. "For hours at a time, sometimes. It's not much fun."

That evening, as I wiped down the table and hung up my apron, I looked about me at the clean, quiet, warm kitchen and thought perhaps, that once, I'd got the better end of the deal. The evening had been fairly calm, with only the servants' meal to make, and Mrs Watling, Doris and I had easily tackled that between the three of us. I glanced at the clock – only twenty minutes past nine. I would be able to have a few precious hours to myself in our room, finishing off reading *Voyage of the Heart* and perhaps making a start on my own play. I stretched luxuriously, yawned, switched off the main light and made my way to the stairs, feeling rather content.

Chapter Eighteen

TRUE TO HIS WORD, TOMMY sent two tickets to the dress rehearsal of the pantomime round to us that week, and Verity and I both arranged our next evening off to coincide with the performance. Tommy had enclosed a note with the tickets and Verity read it silently as I looked at the tickets, hugging the knowledge to my heart that I had a nice evening out to look forward to. It seemed like a long time since my last bit of time off. I thought for a moment of Inspector Marks and whether he and his men had interviewed Ethel yet, and if they had, whether they'd found out anything interesting or useful. For a moment, I almost fell into a reverie of fantasising that what Ethel had to tell them cracked the case and Inspector Marks called again specially, just to thank me for finding such an important witness and said that the case couldn't have been solved without me...

Somehow I managed to pull myself back to reality. I was not going to *think* about this case anymore; hadn't I told myself that? *It was not my business.* I sighed and it was then I realised that Verity had tears in her eyes.

"What's wrong?" I asked, anxiously.

Verity sniffed. "Oh, it's nothing, it's just Tommy. I can tell he's still feeling awfully down about Aldous – and I suppose about *Voyage of the Heart* being cancelled. I mean, it's not like him, this melancholia. He's just not like that, normally."

"Well, it has been a very hard time," I said cautiously but sympathetically. "Aldous was his friend. He's bound to miss him."

Verity sniffed again and then shook her head and put her shoulders back. "Yes, I know. Well, I can't keep moping all day either. Let's look forward to our night at the pantomime and say no more about it."

As was usual when one had something to look forward to, the days between the present and the pantomime seemed to drag terribly. Every day seemed like an endless round of waking up, rubbing the sleep from one's eyes, dragging oneself downstairs, cooking breakfasts, clearing up, cooking luncheon, clearing up, cooking dinner, clearing up... Dorothy had two evening soirées that week, which meant a whole lot more work than usual. I looked to see if the Honourable Cleo Maddox was attending either but her name didn't appear. Despite my resolution to myself, I couldn't help but read the newspaper every day, cover to cover if I got a chance, but nothing about the Connault murder or Aldous Smith's suicide appeared. It was probably just as well, as further news would have tempted me from my resolution to forget the case entirely.

All in all, it was with some relief – not to mention joyous anticipation – that Verity and I found ourselves on an omnibus heading towards Fulham one Tuesday evening, off to see Tommy in *Cinderella*. It was only a few weeks until Christmas and I was glad to be seeing a pantomime. I was in the mood for something silly and frivolous and lighthearted.

Eventually the swaying omnibus pulled up at our stop. We stepped down carefully and, arm in arm, made our way towards the theatre. It was a much smaller building than the Connault and I wondered if it made Tommy sad to have 'come down' in terms of theatrical importance. I spared another thought about Christmas as we made our way to the entrance. There had only been two Christmases at Dorothy's establishment since the events of Merisham Lodge but they had both been rather grim, subdued affairs. Of course, Verity and I hadn't expected to have any time off on the actual day itself and we hadn't had it; after Dorothy had been put to bed that night, the servants had all gathered for a late night drink around the range in the kitchen. That had been quite jolly, I supposed. And, to be fair, Dorothy had given us all presents, proper presents that were a pleasure to receive. I remembered some of my previous places of work, where the gentry had made such a show of handing over presents to the servants on a Christmas morning and how the anticipated parcels had turned out to be something completely functional and disappointing. One particular low had been when I'd been given some material with which to make up a new uniform. On my own expense! At least Dorothy was generous and thoughtful in that way; she'd given me some beautiful silk stockings and a lovely brooch last year. I wondered what I might receive this year.

We handed our tickets over to the door manager and climbed the stairs. We were in the Gods again, of course, but I didn't let that bother me. It was still a wonderful treat to see a show for free.

It wasn't until we actually took our seats that I began to feel uneasy. The Gods were busy and by some odd coincidence, we were sat in the same place we'd been that night at the Connault. It was so busy there wasn't the option to move. I cast a nervous glance at the seat on the end of the row in front of us, a glance that grew even more anxious when I realised that the man sat in it bore quite a startling resemblance to Gideon Bonnacker. I blinked and looked again. Then I nudged Verity. "Doesn't that man look like the – the man who was killed?"

Verity looked and frowned. "Not much. It's just a coincidence, Joan."

"But—" I looked around me at the packed seats and then down at the waiting stage, not sure of quite why I was so uneasy.

"Shh – it's starting."

I tried to settle back in my seat as the curtain went up. Even so, I found myself casting jittery nervous glances about me. Everyone else was riveted on the shenanigans going on on stage. You're being foolish, I told myself, but I could not make myself relax. I watched the Dame come on stage to start singing something full of innuendo, and try as I might, I could not find this sight of a man dressed up grotesquely in women's clothing amusing.

Light shone from the corridor outside as a couple of latecomers came in, bending forward in that way that people have when they're trying to find their seats in the darkness. One was a woman with a cloche hat on and the light from the stage gleamed from the jewellery around her throat.

I gasped. For a moment, I was actually *back* there in the Connault, on the night of the murder, aware of the mysterious woman taking her seat behind the man that she – surely – had killed. It was as if the blurred recollection I'd had was burned away, leaving the memory sharp and clear. Somewhere, deep down inside, I had seen her face and now – sitting in the raucous dark of the Fulham Broadway theatre, I *remembered*. I remembered the minutest glimpse I'd had of her face, the sharp cheekbones and the rosebud lips...

I sat there as if transfixed to the seat. The memory of what I'd actually seen faded once more but that didn't matter. I *knew*. I knew who that woman was. My eyes went back to the stage and there was the confirmation again. Now I knew, it seemed so obvious...

Dazzled by the revelation, the pantomime passed completely unheeded. I sat there in my seat, as if turned to stone. I knew who that woman was now, but why? And how? And, once more, *why*?

At the interval, Verity turned to me. "Want to get some fresh air for five minutes?" I didn't answer, still staring ahead and wondering. "Joan? What's wrong?"

I sighed and brought myself back to reality. "Nothing. I'm just thinking."

Verity gave me a puzzled glance. "Are you going to let me in on the secret?"

I sighed once more and brought my gaze around to hers. "Not yet, V. Not yet. I'm still puzzling things out."

Verity's puzzlement grew more extreme. "Puzzling what out?"

"I don't know yet," I said. I could tell my voice was far away, almost as if I were speaking out of a dream. "That's what I'm puzzling out."

Verity snorted. "Well, suit yourself. I'll be back at the second bell."

"Very well." Normally I would have hated being on my own for the interval, but right now, I didn't care. I just wanted to sit and think and see if I could work it all out. I saw the couple who had come in late leave the Gods along with most of the rest of the audience. They looked very ordinary. The woman wasn't sinister at all, and her face bore no resemblance to the one that I now remembered from that night at the Connault. I pondered the strange ways of the brain and what a mystery its workings were.

I sat there without moving for the entire interval. Normally I would have at least gone off to spend a penny, or to stretch my legs, but neither of those things seemed very important. What I *really* wanted to do was to go home, so I could find Tommy's copy of *Voyage of the Heart*. I felt a little thrill of pride as I realised something. Hadn't I always said that the crime was something to do with the theatre?

There was little chance of returning home early though, not with the whole cast and crew and their friends and relations in the audience, who were prepared to celebrate the first successful run through of the show. I murmured to Verity after the final curtain call that perhaps we should be thinking of going. She gave me an incredulous look.

"Go *now*? Without even saying hello to everyone?"

"I've got an early start tomorrow—" I began to protest but she talked over me, rather crossly.

"You can't even be bothered to say thank you to Tommy for the tickets? Really, Joan, what's got into you?"

"Oh yes." That did pull me up a bit. It would be the height of ingratitude and rudeness just to slope off now without a by-your-leave to the people who'd made it possible for us to attend the show in the first place. I saw that now. And, I realised with a leap of excitement, there might be an opportunity to find out something else that supported my new theory.

"You're quite right," I told Verity firmly, and she looked relieved. "Of course we must say hello and thank you. Come on, let's walk down there now."

Chapter Nineteen

DESPITE BEING A SMALLER THEATRE than the Connault, the Fulham Broadway had a bigger backstage area. It was, however, just as chaotic as it had been when Verity and I had been backstage at the Connault – more so, in fact, because so many of the actors and actresses had had visitors in the audience that night who had come backstage to see them.

As we struggled through the crowd, looking for Tommy, I glanced around, wondering whether Caroline Carpenter would be there. I wasn't surprised when I couldn't see her; she hadn't been in the pantomime and she was getting married in less than a fortnight, if I remembered correctly. Perhaps Verity and I had been one of the last people to ever actually see her act on stage. That made me feel sad, to reflect on how so much talent could just be thrown away.

"Verity, Verity—" Tommy was calling to us from the back of the room. "Over here." We forged our way through the crowds and up to him. He was still wearing his Buttons costume and was sweating quite heavily in the warmth of the room, which made his greeting kiss on the cheek slightly less pleasant than usual. I was still pleased to see him though, although I could see what Verity meant when she said he had changed. Some of the vitality that used to be so apparent had dimmed. I hoped it hadn't gone forever.

We chatted – or rather shouted at each other above the din – discussing the pantomime and the audience and the theatre gossip. In the noise and confusion, my revelation of earlier had paled a little. I now wasn't sure whether I'd remembered correctly or not. Had my mind just thrown up an image that wasn't actually a real memory? Had I actually remembered falsely? I couldn't wait to get back to the relative peace and quiet of our room so I could look at the play and work out whether my suspicions were correct.

"Hullo, Miss Hart," said a familiar voice at my shoulder. I turned to find Gwen Deeds smiling at me. I smiled back and shook hands.

"Do call me Joan, Miss Deeds."

She laughed. "Well then, do call me Gwen."

We chatted pleasantly for a bit. If I'd remembered Gwen, it had been the bitterness in her voice that had stuck with me when she was talking about Caroline and about some women have all the luck. But I'd forgotten that she could also be good company, warm and funny as well. Even so, after ten minutes or so, the conversation began to drift once more into the slightly malicious. Even though it was guiltily amusing, I could tell that Gwen was the sort of person that you don't entrust with your secrets.

In the end, it was I who brought Caroline into the conversation. "So, Miss Carpenter is getting married next week, is that right?"

Gwen's eyes lit up with spiteful glee. "Oh, yes. It's going to be an enormous do, apparently. Saint Paul's, no less. Well, you can't imagine her going for the little local church, can you? Not our Caroline."

I smiled inwardly. "Will there be many people from the theatre there?"

Gwen sniffed. "Not likely. I suppose *Tommy* may get an invitation. I can't imagine she'll want many of this motley crew there. Doesn't quite send the right message, does it? Not for the new role she'll be playing."

"New role?" For a moment I felt glad that perhaps Caroline Carpenter wouldn't be giving up her acting career after all.

Gwen soon put me right. "Lady of the manor, that'll be *her* new role." She sniffed again and added, cattily "I'm sure she'll be just *marvellous* at it."

I was growing tired of the malevolence. It was briefly amusing but after a while, you just felt a bit dirty. I opened my mouth to change the subject when Gwen added, "I can't imagine Caroline will be getting too flustered about being married. It's not like she hasn't done it before."

"Really?" I asked, fascinated. "Caroline – I mean, Miss Carpenter – she's been married before?"

Gwen looked both gleeful and sly. "Oh yes, she has. A long time ago now."

"How do you know? Did she tell you?"

Gwen giggled. "I was helping her unpack at her lodgings this one time. Years ago, now. I saw her marriage certificate – well, just a glimpse of it before she snatched it away. 'Goodness,' I said, 'are you married, Caroline? Whoever to?' and she looked cross as a cat and said she had been once but no longer, thank goodness."

"Who was she married to?"

Gwen looked regretful. "I don't know. I didn't see the name and she got it away from me too quickly. She wouldn't tell me."

"No?"

"No. I got the impression she was a bit ashamed of it, to be honest. Probably something rather hasty, if you see what I mean." She raised her eyebrows at me as if I should know what she meant, which I did, a little, without knowing her exact meaning.

"Joan!" I looked up to see Verity waving at me. "It's nearly eleven o'clock. We have to go or Mrs Anstells will have our hides."

"Golly, I'd hate to be a servant," Gwen said, and

this time she didn't sound catty, she merely sounded sincere.

"It's not that bad," I said, wondering who I was trying to fool. I was happy to go, anyway; I'd had my fill of gossip and slander, and I really wanted to get home to see if my previous suspicions were correct. That reminded me of something. "Gwen, do you remember you lost a costume? Not that long ago? You thought somebody had stolen it?"

Gwen's face, which had been frowning through the first part of my speech, cleared. "Oh yes, that. I remember. I found it right at the back of a cupboard."

"What kind of costume was it?"

Gwen gave me a puzzled look. "What do you mean?"

"I mean, what was it? What role?" I held my breath. If it had been a lion suit, for example, or a suit of armour, then perhaps my theory was utterly wrong.

"Oh, I see. Oh, it wasn't anything special, actually. That's why I couldn't understand someone pinching it. It was just a female outfit for one of the chorus, that's all. Just a coat and hat and a bit of jewellery."

I closed my eyes briefly, breathing out. I had been right, then. Why did I never trust my own judgement? "Thank you, Gwen."

I must have sounded oddly heartfelt because she gave me a strange look and muttered "That's all right."

I shook myself mentally and said goodbye properly. Then I went over to say goodbye to Tommy.

"You were brilliant, Tommy. Thanks so much for the tickets."

Tommy smiled. "You're welcome, my dear. Oh, by the way, you two, are you free next Wednesday night?"

Verity and I looked at each other and shrugged, ruefully. "Unlikely," I said.

"Possibly," Verity said.

"Well, do be free if you can be. We're having farewell drinks for Caroline at the Connault. Just a few backstage, to say goodbye." Tommy looked downcast for a moment. "It'll be a bit of a wake for Aldous as well."

I hesitated. "I'd love to come, Tommy, but I'm not sure if I can. I will try."

Verity nodded her agreement.

"Oh, by the way," I asked, more out of curiosity than anything else. "Did Caroline send you an invitation for her wedding?"

Tommy half-smiled. "She did, actually. Kind of her, although I'm not sure I'll go. I'll be a complete fish out of water there amongst all those highborn folk." He got up and fished about in the pocket of a jacket hanging up on the wall. "Here you are. The very thing itself."

I took it, looking at it curiously. It was very much as I expected, heavy cream card and lots of twirly gilt lettering but on turning it over I could see Caroline had written in a flowing hand *Do come, Tommy darling. Love, C.*

"It was kind of her," Tommy said again, sounding as though he was trying to convince himself. I handed the invitation back to him.

"Come along, Joan," said Verity. "Mrs Anstells will have our hides if we're late. Sorry, Tommy, but we *must* go."

"Very well, my darlings. I'll hope to see you there on Wednesday. Have a safe trip home." There were kisses all round and then Verity and I took our leave.

I MUST HAVE BEEN UNCHARACTERISTICALLY silent on the way home because, as we rounded the corner into our street, Verity drove a sharp elbow into my ribs.

"Ow!"

"Well, honestly, Joan. You've been like a deaf-mute all the way home. What is wrong with you this evening?"

I rubbed my side, slightly annoyed. "I've just been thinking, that's all. You should try it sometime."

Verity gave me a look but didn't rise to my bait. "What have you been thinking about?"

"Lots of things." We had reached the basement railings by now and began to descend the steep steps carefully. Whenever you got back late, there was always a slight nerve-wracking moment where you wondered whether Mr Fenwick had already locked the kitchen door. He never had, so far, but what would I do if he had?

As it happened, he hadn't locked the kitchen door, of course. We slipped inside and made our way upstairs as quietly as we could. Once we were safely in our room, I divested myself of my coat and hat and sat down on the bed.

"I know who killed the man at the Connault Theatre."

Verity stopped dead, her hands to her hat. She took them off slowly and lowered them to her sides. "Guido Bonsignore? You know who killed him?"

"Gideon Bonnacker," I corrected her. "And yes, I think I do."

Verity's eyes were wide. She asked the obvious question. "Well, who, for goodness' sake?"

I shook my head. I felt a bit mean keeping it back but I still didn't know why. "Sorry, V, I can't tell you. Not yet."

Verity snorted. "What?"

"I'm sorry. I don't know enough myself yet. I can't tell anyone yet, not even Inspector Marks."

"For goodness' sake, Joan. You can't even give me a hint?"

I shook my head regretfully. "Actually, I'm sorry I mentioned it. Sorry."

Verity looked daggers. "You are impossible, Joan," she said coldly and stalked from the room, her shoulders rigid.

I felt bad but what could I do? As yet, I only had the theory and one tiny bit of evidence. I wasn't going to make a fool of myself by making a big announcement that could well turn out to be wrong. Thinking of that, and as late as it was, I turned to the copy of *Voyage of the Heart* on my bedside table and opened it, quickly turning to the part of the play that I needed. I tried to think back to what Inspector Marks had told me about the time of death. I read on, nodding to myself. Yes, that tallied. Just about. That was possible.

By the time Verity came back from the bathroom, still in high dudgeon, I was undressed and in bed, my face turned to the wall. I heard her hesitation before getting into her own bed, even heard her take the start of a deep breath, and forestalled any more questions by saying clearly, "I'm sorry, V. Forget I mentioned it, please? I'll tell you everything when I can."

Verity's only response to this could only be written as 'humph'. Then she got into her bed and turned out the light without saying goodnight.

Chapter Twenty

VERITY WAS STILL A LITTLE cool with me the next morning. I couldn't let it worry me. For some reason, Dorothy had decided to have a lunchtime drinks soiree followed by a small dinner party of several of her close chums, and Mrs Watling and I were kept too busy to worry about Verity's moods. I did feel a little guilty. Why had I even mentioned it? I should have just kept my mouth shut. As I made the mushroom and rabbit tartlets, I thought back to our team work at Merisham Lodge – how we'd both played a part in ensuring there was justice. This time around, I knew Verity had had too much on her mind, what with Tommy and Aldous and Dorothy, to be quite as invested in solving the case as I was.

I realised how quickly I'd changed my mind – from telling myself the case was nothing to do with me, to a fever of impatience to get the evidence that would back up my theory. But how was I going to do that? All I had was the a stolen costume and the timings of a part in a play. It sounded pretty thin to me. And the most glaring fact of all was that I didn't know *why*. Where was the motive?

I tried to think it through once again as I worked but it was hopeless –the dishes I was constructing couldn't be done mindlessly or thoughtlessly. I had to give them my full attention or risk both Mrs Watling's and Dorothy's displeasure. I thrust all thoughts of the Connault case to the back of my mind and turned my attention to the job in hand. It was hard not to feel resentful at the lack of time to think but I supposed I should have been used to it by now.

Verity was assisting Nancy and Margaret in serving the food at Dorothy's afternoon party, and all three girls kept whisking in and out of the kitchen to carry up the trays of *amuse bouches* and *hors d'eouvres*. Mr Fenwick kept hurrying back and forth from the wine cellar, although it was bottles of brandy, vodka and whisky that he kept taking up. I supposed they were on the cocktails up there and wondered rather pruriently whether Dorothy was behaving herself or was getting sozzled again.

Finally, the last tray had been carried up, and Mrs Watling, Doris and I had a short moment of peace and quiet before the party ended and the washing up to be done began to come back down. Efficient woman that she was, Mrs Watling had already begun preparing the evening meal for the dinner party, so at least that was underway. Thankfully, I put the kettle on the hob and prepared us all a good cup of tea.

Sitting down on one of the chairs by the range, I sipped my tea and tried to think. If my memory of the face of the woman in the theatre was correct, and now I was convinced it was, then I had a theory – a good theory, given the two pieces of evidence I possessed. But for the life of me, I couldn't work out the motive. Was there any point in going to Inspector Marks when I didn't know why the murder had been committed? Was there any possible way to find out? But how could I go anywhere, or find out anything, when my next afternoon off wasn't for another week? I wouldn't even get to go to the farewell drinks for Caroline Carpenter. I drained the last dregs of my tea, feeling cross and frustrated, a mood not helped by the fact that our brief period of respite was over, and I had to get up and start work again.

Verity came clomping down an hour later with a tea tray in her hands, piled with dirty dishes. I waited until she carried it into the scullery and then darted in after her.

"How was it?"

For a moment I thought she was still sulky with me because she took a second or two to answer, but after a moment I could see she was just tired – tired and worried. "The food was fine, Joan. Thank you."

"I didn't mean that." I took the tray out of her hands, worried she would drop it, she looked so exhausted. "I mean, how was Dorothy? Was she – did she—"

"Did she get completely drunk, you mean, don't you Joan? Yes, of course she did. I've just put her to bed to try and get her to sleep it off before her guests start arriving for the evening."

"Oh, Lord. Do you think she will?"

Verity rubbed her eyes. "I don't know. What am I going to tell them if she won't wake up in time?"

"Could you not say she's unwell?"

"Well, that might work, except some of them coming tonight were here this afternoon. They'll know she's just mightily hungover. And if I don't get it right, what's Dorothy going to do when she finally comes round and all her friends are laughing at her?"

I could hear the helplessness in her voice and felt a surge of anger at Dorothy, for being so weak-willed and selfish. But what could Verity and I do?

"I'll make up some really strong coffee," I suggested. "Later on. And we'll make sure there's some lovely appetisers if people have to wait a little while. Surely we can get her up in time for her to just be a bit fashionably late?"

Verity gave me a look that was half hopeful, half despairing. "Well, it's all we can do, Joanie. I can't think of anything else."

185

I began to sort the dishes out in preparation for washing them. "Why don't you sit through in the kitchen and have a cup of tea? Rest for five minutes?"

"Yes, I will. I feel dead on my feet and the day's not half over yet." She smiled at me rather wanly and turned to leave. Then she turned back. "Listen, Joanie, sorry I was a bit crotchety with you earlier. I've had all these worries about Dorothy on my mind and I felt – oh, I don't know – I felt a bit as if you were leaving me out."

I smiled back, relieved. "Well, I'm sorry to have kept you in the dark. I won't any longer because I need your help."

Verity brightened. "Really?"

"Yes. Look, I know it's going to be a late night tonight for both of us, but let's see if we can stay awake long enough to talk at bedtime."

"Very well." Verity gave a small chuckle. "It might not be such a late one after all. If Dorothy overdoes it again, it could all be over by ten o'clock."

I couldn't help but laugh, although I felt a little cruel doing so at another woman's misfortune. But I felt lighter, more cheerful, after Verity and I had worked out our little spat.

Verity waved to me and left the scullery. I set to the washing up with a will and it didn't seem like such hard work all of a sudden.

As luck would have it, the evening didn't finish at ten o'clock but it wasn't so very late for an evening party. I was in bed by midnight, and Verity came in about ten minutes after that.

"Golly," she said, flopping down on the bed. The bedsprings chimed musically beneath her. "I'm glad tomorrow's going to be quiet."

"It went much as expected then?"

Verity rolled her eyes. "I don't think Dorothy had sobered up *at all*. She just topped herself up. Luckily everyone else was drinking quite heavily so perhaps it wasn't very noticeable..." She trailed away, staring at the floor. "I don't know how long she can go on like this."

I didn't know either. Looming up with grim inevitability was the time that Verity was going to have to ask for help from Mr Fenwick or Mrs Anstells, or both.

Verity sighed and got to her feet with difficulty. She began to undress with fumbling fingers. I wondered whether now was a good time to tell her my theory about the Connault Theatre killer after all. Would it ruin the night's sleep for her when she so obviously needed it?

I pondered this in the time Verity went off to the bathroom to wash and brush her teeth. I was still thinking, unsure of what to do, when she came back.

It was she who actually asked me. "So, Joan, you were going to tell me?"

"Tell you?" I asked, as if I didn't know what she was talking about. Cowardly of me.

"Yes, you noodle. Tell me about who you thought did the murder."

I was silent for a moment. Then I said slowly "It's only a theory. And I barely have any evidence. And I don't know why they did it."

Verity frowned. "You don't know why they did it?"

"No. That's just it. It doesn't make sense to me at the moment. I've been wracking my brains to try and think of a motive."

Now it was Verity's turn to fall silent. She stared down at the tumbled counterpane on her lap for so long I wondered whether she'd actually fallen asleep with her eyes open.

After about five minutes, I said tentatively, "V? Are you all right?"

Verity blinked and came back to life. She looked over at me with an expression I couldn't decipher. Was it – was it *fear*?

"V?" I said again, uneasily.

"Joan—" She stopped herself. It occurred to me then, why hadn't she asked me outright who I thought it was? She cleared her throat and asked "What are your pieces of evidence?"

I pleated the blanket between my fingers. "Well, I hardly have any, to be honest. But I'll tell you what I know." I went on to detail the little that I did know; the stolen costume that Gwen had reported, the timings of particular scenes in the play. Without naming whoever it was that I believed was the killer, it sounded even thinner than I'd anticipated, and I started to stumble over my words, particularly when I saw the sceptical look on Verity's face. The scepticism was mingled with something like relief. Why was she relieved?

"There is one other thing," I added, almost mumbling.

"What's that?"

"It's just – well – I saw her. Her face."

"Whose face? The murderer's?"

I nodded. Verity bit her lip.

"Why didn't you tell the police that, then?" she asked, not unreasonably.

"Because I didn't realise I *had* seen her face. It was almost as if I'd forgotten it and one night – the night at the pantomime, actually – it suddenly came back to me. Like a memory I'd forgotten."

"At the pantomime?" The note of fear was back in Verity's voice.

"Yes. It was like a sudden flash, as if my mind had brought back the memory I'd forgotten."

There was silence as we stared at one another. I thought Verity was going to ask me something else but after a moment, she said, in quite an artificial voice. "Joan, do you mind if we talk about this another time? I'm just about all in."

"That's fine," I said, slightly hurt and perhaps a bit disappointed. But what could I say?

189

Verity gave me a slight smile. Then she said, "Goodnight, then," and turned and lay down in her bed, turning her head away from me and closing her eyes.

I stared at her for a moment, half wanting to take her up on whatever was bothering her. But after a moment, I too lay down in bed. I turned off the bedside light and lay there in the darkness, wide-eyed and wondering.

Chapter Twenty One

I DON'T KNOW WHETHER I EXPECTED Verity to change her mind about wanting to know who I thought the killer was but she didn't. The subject just didn't come up between us again. The next day was quiet in terms of our workload, thankfully, with just Dorothy's and the servants' usual meals to prepare. Ironically, now that I didn't really need it, I had more time to think. I had hoped that my conversation with Verity would have brought me new insight, helped me see with fresh eyes, but that hadn't happened. For some reason, she'd cut me off and that was another mystery.

That evening the servants were having kedgeree, quite an easy dish to make. I carefully lifted the eggs into boiling water with a teaspoon and turned the egg timer on the dresser over so I knew when they'd be hardboiled. The kitchen was filling up with steam and I went over to the window to open it a little. It was a grey, cold day, with the odd squall of sleet occasionally darkening the pavements.

I'd expected to see more of Verity that day, given that Dorothy was likely to stay in bed until late and probably spend the afternoon on the chaise-longue in the drawing room in the front of the fire. I stretched and eased the ache in my back, feeling that old familiar feeling of envy. What I wouldn't give for hours and hours of emptiness, of time to be filled however I wanted it to be. I was quite sure I would have been able to solve this Connault case if only I'd been given enough time to think.

As it was, I barely saw Verity. She didn't come down for supper but asked for a tray to be sent up to Dorothy's bedroom. I frowned as Nancy delivered the message. Was Verity trying to avoid me? Nancy was waiting expectantly for my answer. "That's fine," I said, thinking about things. "I'll bring it up, don't you worry. Go in, Nancy, and have something to eat."

Dinner on nights where Dorothy wasn't entertaining was a less formal affair than it might have been. Of course, we still looked to Mr Fenwick and Mrs Anstells for permission but we sat next to whom we pleased and we were allowed to chat as we ate. I had been hoping that Verity would come down so I could talk to her, but as she wasn't going to, I was going to have to corner her myself. Was it possible that she was trying to avoid me? Why?

As I climbed the stairs to Dorothy's room, I pondered it uneasily. Was it something I had done to offend her? Something I had said? I wracked my brains as I shifted the tray about in my hands, trying to open the bedroom door, but nothing came to mind. Was it just that she was bored with my constant musings on who might have been the Connault killer? Or did she think I was overstepping the mark and should leave well enough alone?

I'd spent so long trying to balance the tray with getting the door open that eventually Verity opened it herself. She looked – yes, she did – startled to see me.

"Hello, thought I'd bring this up myself," I said.

She didn't look very pleased although she thanked me. "Just leave it over there, Joan. Thank you."

I did so. There was an awkwardness between us that had never been there before, and I couldn't think of why that would be. "I thought you might come down to eat with us," I said, unsure of whether to take her up on it.

"I didn't feel like it tonight. I'm too tired."

"Oh." Another heavy silence fell. To hell with it, I thought, and threw caution to the wind. "Is something wrong?"

"No," Verity said coldly.

I frowned. "Then why are you acting like this?"

"I'm not acting like anything, Joan."

"Yes you are."

"No, I'm not."

"But—" I stopped, frustration strangling me. I knew Verity though – she could be as stubborn as any mule. If she didn't want to tell me what was bothering her, she wouldn't.

I swallowed and gathered my courage. "It is something I've done?"

Verity made a noise of impatience. "There's nothing *wrong*, Joan. Don't keep on about it. I'm just very fatigued. It's been a fairly awful week."

We stood for a moment, looking at one another. Half of me wanted to carry on, to have a proper argument and at least get what was bothering her out of her system and into the open, but after a minute, I sighed and turned away. I didn't have the energy for a quarrel.

"Very well. Just ring down when you've finished and one of the girls will collect your tray."

"Thank you," she said, but very formally, as if I were a stranger. I shook my head, wanting her to see my frustration, and then left without saying goodbye.

WELL, THAT MADE FOR A bit of a gloomy evening, I can tell you. I went back downstairs and sat down for dinner but ate the kedgeree as if it were cardboard – I couldn't taste a thing. Doris and I cleared the kitchen and washed up, while Mrs Watling went through the order sheets for tomorrow. All the time, I was thinking about Verity and wondering what was on her mind. Could it be Dorothy and her drinking? Was that worry enough to cause Verity to act the way she was?

I could have done with a drink myself that night, to be honest. Of course, I didn't have one. I made myself a cup of cocoa, said goodnight to Doris and Mrs Watling, and carried it up to bed with me. I fully expected Verity to be in our room, perhaps already asleep as she'd said she was so exhausted. But she wasn't there. I stood for a moment in the doorway, frowning.

I drank my rapidly cooling cocoa, undressed, washed and brushed my teeth. I was tired but I didn't think I would be able to sleep just yet, despite my fatigue. There were too many thoughts running around in my head, too many emotions running around in my heart. I brushed out my hair in front of the mirror, expecting to hear Verity's footsteps in the corridor outside any moment, but she didn't come.

Climbing into bed, I thought that I would read for a little while. Hopefully a good book would distract me, help me calm my thoughts and prepare myself for sleep. But I realised I was without a novel, or at least without one I'd not already read several times before. I made a sound of annoyance. I thought, briefly, that this would be a good opportunity to do some writing of my own, but I didn't feel like it.

I doubted I would be able to write anything down that was worth re-reading.

The nearest book to me was *Voyage of the Heart*, lying on the bedside table. But I'd already read that... I picked it up, idly flicking through it. It was quite a handsome book, with a fly-leaf covering the red leather binding. I flipped through the pages of the play, marvelling again how those black markings on white paper could become real human emotion on the stage. It was like magic, really.

I realised I'd never actually read right to the back of the book and had put it down once I'd reached the end of the actual play. I did so now, leafing through the mostly blank pages until I got to the very back cover. Then I realised there was something tucked into the flyleaf at the back, a slip of paper.

It was hard to remove. I tried grasping it with my fingernails but it stubbornly resisted. In the end, I had to get up and find Verity's eyebrow tweezers before I could grab a corner and pull it free. I opened up the paper curiously. I think I had thought for one giddy moment that it could be money and was already thinking of how I could return it to Tommy, if that was the case.

But of course, it wasn't money. It was just a handwritten note, a flowing hand on cream coloured paper, and all it said was *Darling, meet me at eleven tonight, my place.*

I frowned. Where had I seen that handwriting before? It wasn't Tommy's, or at least I didn't think so. I read the note again. *Darling, meet me at eleven tonight, my place.* Was it a lover's note? Or something more prosaic. Eleven o'clock at night – surely a little more suggestive? Or was that just me being suspicious? And what business was it of mine, anyway?

I folded the note back up and put it back in the flyleaf. Then, thinking I should just check, I turned to the front cover and checked the flyleaf there, in case there was another note. There wasn't, but there was something else I noticed. Written in pencil on the front page, in tiny writing at the bottom were the words *Aldous Smith*.

I frowned again. Wasn't this Tommy's book? He was the one who'd given it to me, after all. Or had he grabbed Aldous's copy by mistake one time and either not realised or not cared? I didn't think it was very likely that the actors cared much about having their own copies of the play, although of course, I wasn't sure.

Oh, what did it matter anyway? I was very tired now, so tired my eyelids were fluttering. I put the play back on the bedside table and slid down under the bed covers. Normally I would have left the light on for Verity, but I was feeling so cross with her, I couldn't be bothered to do so. Besides, who knew what time she would actually come to bed? I clicked the switch and pulled the covers up to my chin, settling my head on the pillow. I was asleep in moments.

Chapter Twenty Two

THE STAGE WAS ENORMOUS. IT stretched for miles and miles and the red velvet curtains climbed up into the clouds above, disappearing from view. I couldn't see beyond the footlights, which were as dazzling as the sun. I stood there on the boards of the stage, blinking in the light and feeling horribly exposed. I knew I had to perform something, I had to say the words of the play, but nothing was coming to mind. I was dumb as well as blind. Corpsing, I'd heard Tommy call it before.

Corpsing. Funny the way things are called in the theatre.

I stood there on the enormous stage, screwing up my eyes against the dazzle of the footlights. Were they getting brighter? Surely they couldn't get any brighter without blinding me entirely? There was a noise on the edge of hearing that was gradually growing in volume. Was I supposed to be singing? I listened as the noise got louder and louder. It was a babble of voices, male and female, and as I listened, I could hear what they were saying, just words and phrases here and there. *She's done this before, a voyage of the heart, he'd do anything for her, she's done this before, a voyage of the heart, he'd do anything for her...* The golden dazzle of the lights grew ever more bright, and I held my hands up, watching the light penetrate them, lighting up the bones and the blood and above it all, the voices chanted and sang. *She's done this before, she's done this before...*

I woke quite suddenly, my heart hammering. It took a few moments before I realised I was in my bed, the room dark about me with just a thin grey glimmer around the curtains at the window. I lay there, trembling a little. It had seemed so real to me, that stage. And the voices... As I came back to reality, I realised something else. That dream had showed me the truth.

I sat up in excitement. It was then I realised that Verity was in her bed, just a humped figure under the blankets, and breathing steadily. For a moment, I thought of shaking her awake, but I almost immediately dismissed the idea. Now that I knew the truth – or I thought I did – there was only one person I needed to talk to. There was only one person who would be able to tell me if I were being foolish or not.

I groped for the bedside clock and squinted at it in the darkness. A quarter off the hour of six.

Not too early to get up, and besides, I didn't think I could remain in bed, not with my new found knowledge. I felt fizzy with excitement and the need to take action. How early would I be able to call? Would I be able to call from the house telephone or would I need to invent an excuse to go and find a public telephone box? I thought the former would be acceptable, particularly if I could make sure I wasn't overheard.

I got up, gathered up my clothes as quietly as I could, and made my way to the bathroom. It was icy cold in there with the fire out so I washed, shivering, as quickly as I could in cold water, pinned up my hair and dressed, my teeth chattering. Creeping downstairs, I met Nancy, who was bringing up the hot coals to get the fires started, yawning away as if her jaw were on a hinge.

"Oh, hullo, Joan," she said amiably but sleepily.

"Hullo." I had to stop myself from bounding down the stairs. I looked at the grandfather clock in the hallway as I made for the kitchen stairs. *Oh, come on, come on...* Why did time go so slowly when you didn't want it to?

I lit the range, put the kettle on the hob, and began to prepare the breakfast with fingers jittery with impatience. I was starting to worry about whether I would be able to contact Inspector Marks. I knew he was a very busy man, and what if he was out of London, investigating a case elsewhere?

Or taking a holiday? You'll just have to wait and see, I told myself, trying to calm down and failing miserably.

I was never particularly chatty in the mornings so Mrs Watling didn't comment on my silence that morning. She did look a little askance when I burned the first batch of toast but simply folded her lips and said nothing. Cursing inside my head, I cut more slices and put them back on the toasting tray. I kept stealing anxious glances at the clock on the kitchen wall. Nine o'clock was when I was going to attempt to telephone, and I just hoped that wouldn't be too early or too late.

I ate my own breakfast barely tasting a mouthful. Food had never seemed less important. It was baking day today, and I knew Mrs Watling and I would be chained to the kitchen table for the next few hours, so if I were going to make a telephone call it had to be now. Doris was finishing the washing up and Mrs Watling was occupied with the fishmonger's boy, who had just called round with today's order.

At the last moment, I decided that what I had to say to Inspector Marks was so important that I really needed the privacy of a public phone box, if that wasn't a contradiction in terms. Chewing my lip, I wondered how on Earth I was going to get away for long enough to make the call? I knew there was a telephone box at the end of the street, but it would still mean coming up with a convincing cover story. And – a secondary thought occurred to me – did I even have the money for a public call? I hunted out my purse and checked, feeling despair at the findings. I barely had enough money for a minute's call.

I would have to see if I could use the house telephone after all. But the chances of being interrupted or overheard were high. What would people think if they heard what I was intending to say to Inspector Marks? I clenched my fists in frustration.

I was still there, frozen to the spot with indecision, when I felt a finger poke me in the back. I jumped.

"What on Earth is wrong with you?"

Verity sounded more like herself than she had done for the past three days. As I turned to face her, I realised that, whilst we seemed to be at odds for the moment, she *was* my friend, and I could rely on her. I could always rely on her. All of a sudden, the mist of confusion and panic cleared.

"Verity, can you help me?"

Verity had been smiling but at this, her face fell. "What's wrong?" she asked again.

I didn't have time to explain properly. "Can you cover for me? I need to slip out for five minutes."

"*Cover* for you? What, with Mrs Watling?"

"Or whomever asks. And—" I hesitated. "Can you lend me some money?"

Now Verity looked alarmed as well as serious.

"What's *wrong*, Joan?" She began to get that scared look on her face again. "What's going on?"

I shook my head impatiently. "Verity, will you just trust me? I can't tell you everything now, but I need you to help me. Can you help me?"

She stared at me, chewing her lip for a moment. Then, clearly making up her mind, she nodded, slowly. "Yes. Wait here. I'll get my purse."

I waited there, trying not to jig from foot to foot with impatience. I heard her footsteps coming back and hugged my arms across my body. I was too tense to smile at her but I could see that she was holding something in her hand.

"Here, take this." She poured a small heap of coins into my palm. "I'm going to see if Mrs Watling can sit down with me to plan a dinner party that Dorothy wants to give next week. Quite a tricky menu."

"Is it?" I said, interested despite myself.

Verity rolled her eyes. "Bloody hell, Joan, I'm making it up as I go along! Now, go and do whatever you have to do but be quick, I can only keep her talking for so long."

I began to hurry away but just as quickly turned back and hugged Verity in a quick, fierce embrace. "Thank you," I whispered in a heartfelt burst in her ear.

She half-smiled back but she looked suddenly pale and tense. I didn't have time to ask why. Instead I closed my fingers more tightly around the coins she'd given me and scurried up the stairs. I would have to risk using the front door so as not to alert Mrs Watling to my leaving.

My good luck angel must have been with me. I made it out of the front entrance without Mr Fenwick or Mrs Anstells noticing and ran as swiftly as I could down the street to the telephone kiosk. I was shivering, having not wanted to take the time to fetch my coat. Besides, it would make it easier to sneak back without it looking like I'd actually left the house.

The telephone box was empty – another piece of luck. I hoped I wasn't using it all up before I got to speak to Inspector Marks. But no, my angel must have still been with me because after only a couple of tries, I was put through to the inspector's office and his kind voice greeted me pleasantly. He honestly sounded like he was pleased to hear from me.

Now it came down to it, I had a momentary loss of confidence. I didn't really have any evidence, did I? It was intuition and a few overheard scraps of conversation, a role in a play and a missing costume. Not very much to build a prosecution case on, was it?

"Miss Hart? Are you still there?"

I took a deep breath. *Believe in yourself, Joan Hart.* "Yes, sir, I'm still here. I'm calling because I think I know who killed Gideon Bonnacker. No, I *do* know who killed him."

There was a short silence on the other end of the telephone, so I could hear the crackles and whistles of the line. "Indeed," said the inspector's voice. He sounded neutral, but beneath the surface, I could hear that guarded excitement that I remembered from the days at Merisham Lodge. "Well, Miss Hart—"

"Call me, Joan," I said and then blushed.

"Yes, of course. Joan. Well, why don't you tell me all about it?"

Chapter Twenty Three

AFTER I'D PUT THE TELEPHONE down in the kiosk and scurried back to work (successfully managing to get back into the house without anyone noticing I was gone – my good luck angel was working very hard that day), I returned to my chores, feeling – truth to be told – rather flat. Inspector Marks hadn't laughed at me or told me I was being ridiculous; in fact, he'd sounded rather eager to get started uncovering the evidence. But now all I could do was leave it in the hands of the police, while I went back to my tedious, kitchen-bound existence. The washing up seemed endless, that day; there was a never-ending production line of vegetables to be peeled and chopped, meat to be seasoned, biscuits, scones and bread to be baked. I didn't want to do any of it.

I sat down to luncheon in a dim sort of mood. The chances were that that was the absolute last I would have to do with the case. Inspector Marks would (I hoped) find the evidence he needed, make the arrest and then it would be all over the papers for a short while before the world forgot about it and everything went quiet until the trial. I tried to console myself with the fact that I wouldn't have to give evidence at any trial, this time around. Or that I probably wouldn't. It wasn't much consolation.

Verity was equally quiet. We didn't talk at all, except for one short, odd conversation we had out in the corridor after luncheon, when she grabbed my sleeve as I walked past her.

"What is it?" I enquired. "By the way, thank you again so much for helping me this morning."

Verity waved a hand impatiently, as if batting away my thanks. "Joan—" She said my name and stopped abruptly before beginning to speak again.

"What is it?" I asked, interrupting her.

Verity still had hold of my arm. "Joan – you would – you would always do the right thing, wouldn't you?"

This was so unexpected that I just gazed at her. "What do you mean?"

Verity shook her head impatiently. "I mean, you would always do what had to be done. Wouldn't you?"

I half shrugged, not really understanding her meaning. "Well, I would hope so."

She stared at me fixedly a moment longer and then released my sleeve from her hand. She stood back. "I suppose I just have to trust you," she said, stepping back. She said it again, staring into my face as if she could reassure herself. "I suppose I just have to trust you."

Lost for words, I stared at her. She gave me one last, searing glance and turned on her heels and began to climb the stairs, her head down, as if all her energy were draining away.

PUZZLED AND ANXIOUS, I WENT back to the kitchen. I worked the afternoon's tasks in something of a dream, thoughts of Verity and Inspector Marks competing for who could make my head more of a whirl. It was a relief to get to dinner, to have Dorothy's food taken up for her alone, and to sit at the servants' table amongst people who, although I couldn't exactly say they were friends, at least were familiar and safe and didn't demand anything much of me emotionally. Verity wasn't there – she must have been dining with Dorothy.

It was Doris's evening off, and I had a pile of washing up awaiting me. Philosophically, I began to carry everything through to the scullery and to run the water into the sink.

I could hear voices outside in the kitchen; Mrs Watling's and a deeper one. I held my breath, suddenly taut with anticipation. Then, because I couldn't wait any longer, I hurried to the scullery door and peered out. My stomach jumped. Inspector Marks was there, talking to Mrs Watling.

"Ah, Miss Hart," he said as soon as he saw me. "I've been asking Mrs Watling here for permission for you to accompany me this evening."

I could feel the blush start up in my face. Then I realised, from the look on his face, that he wasn't talking about a purely social invitation. The blush receded and excitement leapt up in my throat. I looked at Mrs Watling and there must have been desperation in my eyes because she threw up her hands and said, in a scolding voice than nonetheless carried some affection in it, "I'm sure I don't know what the world's coming to. But if the inspector needs you, Joan, then I suppose go you must."

I bobbed a curtsey to her out of sheer gratitude. It was then I realised I was dressed in my two-day-old, soiled uniform.

"May I be allowed to go and change my clothes, sir?" I asked, wondering if that was an indelicate question.

The inspector didn't look scandalised. "Yes, but be as quick as you can."

I didn't need telling twice. I pelted for the stairs and took them two at a time, arriving at my room in a breathless heap. I pushed open the door and was startled to see Verity, standing there dressed in her coat and hat and pulling on her gloves.

"Are you going out?" I asked in some confusion.

Verity looked extremely tense. For a moment I thought she wasn't going to answer me. "I'm coming with you," she said, eventually.

"With me?" Shock made me ungrammatical.

"With you and Inspector Marks."

Shock was piled upon shock. "With us? Why? And where are we going?"

For a moment, I thought Verity was going to cry. "I don't know," she whispered.

I stared at her but only for a moment – I had to get dressed. I tore off my uniform, splashed myself with the cold water from the basin on the dressing table, and quickly pulled on my good blouse and skirt. My hair was a disaster but I didn't have time to fix it. I rammed my hat on my head, picked up my gloves and put my coat on as Verity and I hurried back out of the door.

INSPECTOR MARKS HAD A POLICE car waiting outside – an unmarked one, thankfully, I could just hear the gossip flying around the street if the neighbours had seen us getting into a car with bell and sign on it. We drove through the streets of London, Inspector Marks sitting next to the driver up front, Verity and I hunched tensely in the back seat. I don't believe the three of us exchanged one word on the journey. I wondered where we were going but as we approached the West End, I realised

I knew. I didn't have to ask. I suppose all I had to do was trust Inspector Marks. That made me think about what Verity had said to me earlier. *I suppose I have to trust you*. Was that what this case was all about, after all? Being able to trust another person to do the right thing by you?

THE LIGHTS OF THE CONNAULT Theatre blazed before us. As Inspector Marks handed us out of the car and bent to confer with the driver, I turned to Verity, to ask her something, I'm not sure what. At the sight of her face, I forgot whatever it was I was going to ask. She was milk-pale and trembling.

"V?" I asked tentatively and put a hand out to her but she shook her head and moved away. It occurred to me then to wonder why she was accompanying us. Was it because Inspector Marks thought we worked as a team? The thought pleased me.

If there had been a show on that night at the Connault, it was over. The entrance vestibule was empty and the corridors dark. Inspector Marks walked confidently towards the entrance to the stalls and Verity and I followed him. As we got close to the double doors that led into the theatre, we could hear music and laughter and people's voices. I realised now why we were here.

The actors and crew were on the stage, all sat on chairs that had been drawn up in a big circle, or lounging on some settees and chaise longues which looked like props. Caroline Carpenter sat like a queen to the rear of the circle, dressed in a shimmering silver gown that sparkled under the glow of the stage lights. As we walked closer, I had the incongruous thought that she was supposed to be getting married next week. A winter wedding. As I thought that, a vision of Caroline in her wedding dress rose in my mind's eye – I could see her as clearly as if she were standing there in front of me, dressed in icy white silk, a white fur wrapped around her, the cold shine of the diamonds in her hair and at her throat and ears. It made me feel sad, because I realised I would never get to see it in real life.

It took everyone a while to notice us. Tommy was telling a joke and everyone was laughing. It was Caroline who first realised we were there and I was by then close enough to see something flicker in her gaze as she realised Inspector Marks was climbing the stage steps, Verity and I behind him. Gradually, the laughter around the circle faded and died.

"Good evening," said Inspector Marks genially as he came up to where everyone was sitting.

Tommy was the first to react. "Good evening, Inspector. Erm – like a drink?" He proferred a glass half full with ale. "Or Caroline brought some champagne, if you'd prefer that?"

I saw him look over at Verity anxiously. Her eyes

met his and they exchanged a look that I couldn't decipher.

"Not for me, thank you." The geniality in Inspector Mark's voice fell away. "This isn't a social call."

"It isn't?" Caroline sat up a little but her voice was still the same languid drawl as it always had been. "Whatever do you mean, Inspector Marks?"

There was a short silence. Inspector Marks found a couple of spare chairs and indicated that Verity and I should sit down. Verity did so, almost collapsing into the seat as if the strength had left her legs. Gwen, who was sitting next to her, put a concerned hand out to her, but Verity ignored her, staring at the floor.

I remained standing, next to the inspector. I wanted the advantage of height. Inspector Marks gave me an approving glance.

"I'm here to talk about the murder of the man who was killed here, six weeks ago, during a performance of *Voyage of the Heart*. The name of the victim was reported in the newspapers as that of an Italian citizen called Guido Bonsignore." The inspector let his gaze sweep around the circle of faces. They looked puzzled, worried, intrigued and wary. "That was not his real name," he added.

There was another silence. I had the fanciful thought that the spirit of the theatre was even now infusing the inspector, as I'd once felt it had done to me. He was certainly making the most of some dramatic pauses.

Inspector Marks went on. "The actual name of the murder victim was Gideon Bonnacker."

There were two faces I watched at that revelation. I saw Gwen's eyebrows go up and her mouth make an 'o' shape, as she clearly remembered something she'd thought she'd forgotten. Just as I'd forgotten I'd actually *seen* the murderer. The other face didn't move a muscle. Not even a flicker. But I would have expected nothing less.

"This has been a very strange case," the inspector remarked, walking around the outside of the circle slowly. Heads turned to watch him as he walked. "For a long while, we weren't even sure who the victim was. We had a whole theatre-full of witnesses, all of whom had seen precisely nothing. Before this case, I wouldn't have said it were possible – to have that many people in the vicinity of a murder and for them all to have noticed nothing."

He had come to rest behind Tommy, who was staring ahead of himself uneasily. The inspector stood there for a good few seconds before speaking again. I heard Verity gulp and suddenly realised what had been preying on her mind. I bit my lip.

"As it was, there *was* a witness," said Inspector Marks, quite lightly. I heard the intake of breath around the circle. The inspector's head turned towards me. "Over to you, Miss Hart. Tell us what you saw on the night of the murder, when you and Miss Hunter were seated up there—" He gestured towards the back of the theatre. "Up there in the Gods."

I had been half expecting this, given the theatrics that had just gone on, but still it was my turn to gulp. I stepped forward, literally into the spotlight. I had to clear my throat before I spoke and as I did, I wished I could sound firmer and more confident, just as the inspector did.

"I – I—" I pulled myself together and spoke up. "I was sitting in the row behind Gideon Bonnacker, about three seats away from the end of our row. As the curtain came up on the play, I saw a woman come into our row and sit behind the – the victim."

"Yes, yes, this mysterious woman," said Caroline, sounded irritated. "The one the police could find no trace of. Do you actually have anything concrete to say?"

I swallowed. "The police know that this woman was the murderer. She stabbed Gideon Bonnacker through the back of his chair under the cover of darkness and while everyone was distracted by the play. Then she left before more than a few minutes had elapsed."

"Well?" Caroline demanded.

I drew myself up a little straighter. *The truth shall set you free.* "I know who she was. I actually saw her face."

"And?" Caroline said, in a bored voice.

I cleared my throat. "She was Aldous Smith."

There was more than a gasp this time. There was Caroline's angry exclamation of "Impossible!", Tommy's cry of protest, whispers and hisses carrying around the circle.

"That's enough," said the inspector sharply. "Let Miss Hart speak."

I wished my hands would stop trembling. I tried not to clench them at my sides. "When I say that the woman was Aldous Smith, I mean she was Aldous dressed up as a woman." I addressed Gwen for the next sentence. "He was the one who took that costume, Gwen, and returned it later. He didn't appear in the first act of the play, so there would have been just enough time for him to put on his disguise, go up to the Gods, er – er, stab Mr Bonnacker and then hurry back down to backstage and get rid of the costume, just before he had to appear in his first scene."

There was another silence. I could see people glancing around from face to face, clearly wondering how they were supposed to react to his news.

Caroline was the first to speak. "Why – why, how extraordinary," she said, wonderingly. I watched her clasp her hands together and look into the far distance, as if she were seeking to understand what I'd just told her. "Aldous – Aldous a killer. Who would have thought it? Why on Earth did he do it?"

I was silent. Was this for me to say or should I leave it up to the inspector?

He came to my rescue. He walked on a little further from Tommy, towards Caroline. I heard Verity gulp again, more of a retch than a gulp. I wanted so much to reassure her but at that very moment I couldn't.

"Oh," said the inspector and this time the steel was in his voice. "He wasn't doing it for himself. He had a reason, but it was mostly to do with somebody else."

Again, glances around the circle. Worried faces. I blinked in the glare of the spotlight and, for a moment, my dream of being on the enormous stage came back to me again. I remembered the voices that had sung and chanted. *She's done this before, a voyage of the heart, he'd do anything for her...*

By now the inspector had reached Caroline. She looked up at him with a quizzical expression on her lovely face as he leaned closer in.

"Oh, yes, he had a good reason," said the inspector, looking very steadily at Caroline. "Didn't he, Mrs Bonnacker?"

The silence that followed was so long I could almost hear the woodworm chewing the boards of the stage. It was as if everyone held their breath.

It was Gwen who broke it. "I *knew* I'd seen the name," she said, her voice so loud after the silence that we all jumped. All except Caroline, who sat as if frozen in ice. "I knew I'd seen it before, on that marriage certificate."

"Yes, indeed," said the inspector. He and Caroline were still gazing at one another, as rapt as lovers. "My men found that marriage certificate today when we searched your lodgings, Mrs Bonnacker. I wonder why you kept it? Were you hoping to persuade him to grant you a divorce? He would never have agreed to that, would he, Mrs Bonnacker? Caroline, if I may? He was a devout Catholic."

He stepped back and the hypnotic spell was broken. Caroline looked down at the floor, her face still a neutral mask.

"So," said the inspector. He continued on his slow way around the circle. Half the eyes of the group were following him, whilst half were gazing in horror at Caroline. She continued to look at the floor. I watched the profile of her face, the flawless contours of cheek and nose and chin, and wondered how it was that the outside of someone could be so deceiving.

Tommy spoke up, in a kind of faltering voice I'd never heard him use before. "I don't – I don't understand."

"Don't you, sir? It's quite simple. Very simple, when you look at it. Miss Carpenter here, persuades her lover, Aldous Smith, to murder her husband. Because she won't be able to marry her very rich, very powerful, very influential fiancé, if she's already married, will she? Either that, or she'll have to take the risk of marrying Sir Nicholas Holmes bigamously."

I dared to sneak a glance at Verity and saw to my surprise that her face was buried in her hands. I could only risk a momentary glimpse though, as the inspector continued to speak.

"I think, Caroline, that your husband – that's Gideon Bonnacker – contacted you some months ago. He was back in the country from Italy; rather hard up for money, travelling on a false passport. From what my men have dug up, he seemed to be involved in some pretty shady deals over in Italy. A spot of forgery here, a spot of embezzlement there. So he's not a particularly nice character, is he? A gambler too. Wonder how he squared that with his Catholicism?" The inspector had walked further around the circle so that now he was next to me, looking across to where Caroline sat like an ice-queen, still frozen in one position. "Well, I digress a little. What I think, Caroline, is that he contacted you and began to blackmail you. Little cash payments here and there. We thought he'd won it at the racetrack, but there I think we were wrong. He was bleeding you dry, wasn't he? And it wouldn't have stopped. If you'd married Sir Nicholas as a bigamist, why, then he would have had even more of a hold over you. He had to be stopped, didn't he?"

Caroline looked up at him. Her face was still

blank but there was a spark, deep down in her eyes, which made me shiver.

The inspector patted Verity on the shoulder as he walked past her, but she didn't react. He took no notice, circling the group again to walk closer to where Caroline sat.

"Poor Aldous," said the inspector, softly. "He was very much in love with you, wasn't he? What did you tell him about your upcoming marriage? That you didn't mean to go through with it? That it was just a marriage of convenience and it wouldn't make a difference to the real, the true passion you had for him, Aldous Smith?"

"I *knew* it," Gwen said vehemently, again making us all, save for the inspector and Caroline, jump. "He was absolutely besotted with her, he'd have done anything for her. Oh, how *could* you, Caroline? How could you take advantage of him like that?" I got the impression that Gwen was more upset about Aldous' feelings for Caroline being confirmed than she was about the fact that he had been a murderer.

Caroline got to her feet in one fluid movement, surprising us all. Both the inspector and I tensed. Caroline cast a scornful glance around us all, sweeping us with disdain. "Oh, *shut* up," she said to Gwen, not even deigning to look her in the face. Gwen sagged back in her chair, mouthing her distress.

There was another short silence while Caroline

and Inspector Marks took a tense measure of each other. Then, breaking the gaze, Inspector Marks gestured towards the edge of the stage, where a couple of figures detached themselves from the shadows.

Caroline saw the two uniformed officers approaching, and whilst her reed-straight posture did not change, something happened to her face. It weakened and crumbled, just for a moment, before she flung back her hair and lifted her chin.

The officers had to take her past me towards the right hand stage steps. They hadn't handcuffed her, but were holding her delicate upper arms, one big hand on each side. Caroline wasn't protesting but as she neared me, she slowed and they allowed her to do so. I watched her, tensely, as she came to a halt opposite me. We stared at one another for a long moment.

"What an actress you were," I said. I didn't even know I was going to say it before I did and for once, it came out just right, perfectly pitched: sadness and disbelief there in equal measures.

For a moment I thought she was going to spit in my face. Then, with a shudder of something like pain twisting her face, she turned away and allowed her captors to lead her from the stage, leaving silence behind her.

Chapter Twenty Four

THE SILENCE ONLY LASTED SECONDS, of course. The moment the main doors to the theatre had swung shut behind Caroline and the police officers, the quietness was broken by Verity bursting into racking sobs.

"Verity—" At last I could comfort her. I hurried forward and took her in my arms.

She sobbed for about five minutes, soaking the shoulder of my coat, which I hadn't even had time to remove since we arrived at the theatre. Tommy and Gwen were there, soothing and stroking, and after another storm of tears, the tumult gradually tapered off, eventually leaving Verity drained and gasping.

"I'm sorry," she said, her voice thickened. "I'm just so *relieved*."

"I know." I let her sit up and squeezed her arm as she did so, in sympathy.

"You know?" She opened her mouth to say more, and I shook my head and nodded towards Tommy.

Verity's eyes went wide and she nodded after a moment.

Tommy, Gwen and the rest of the cast and crew were looking both shell-shocked and mystified. Little hisses were leaking from one group of people to another as the truth of what had happened began to filter through. The sound of people's voices, shocked, exclaiming, even – oddly – triumphant, began to rise. People were perhaps realising that it wasn't so very odd after all. They were actors, used to dramatic scenes, used to the power of a good story. It just so happened that, this time, truth had been stranger than fiction.

As the hubbub ebbed and flowed around us, I helped Verity to her feet and looked around for Inspector Marks. He was deep in conversation with Tommy, but as if he felt my gaze, he looked around and nodded, as if he'd heard my unspoken question.

"Let me take you ladies home," he said, coming over to us. Tommy trailed behind him, looking as though he were waking from a not particularly pleasant dream. "It's getting late, and I have a lot of work to do before the morning."

Verity flung her arms around Tommy in a fierce bear-hug and he looked a little taken aback. He kissed the top of her head and released her.

"Come along, V," I said and piloted her towards the stage steps, Inspector Marks following behind.

In the car on the way home, Verity collapsed back against the seat as if she were about to faint. She put her face in her hands momentarily.

"I thought *you* thought it was Tommy," she said, in a voice that suggested she hadn't quite cried out all her tears, yet.

"I know you did." I looked out of the window at the lights and bustle of the pavements of London. "Well, I realised that's what you thought when we were at the theatre. Oh, Verity."

Verity sniffed. "I know, I know. My head's been in such a whirl lately...I don't know what I was *thinking*."

"You were panicking," I said, practically. "And—" I added, to be fair. "If we'd just been able to talk about it – properly, I mean – you would have known there was no possible way Tommy would have done a thing like that. Not to mention it was impossible for him to be off the stage at the time of the murder."

"I know," cried Verity. "It was just that I thought – oh, I thought that—" She broke off abruptly, looking at Inspector Marks who was sitting up front, silent but listening keenly. "I remembered Asharton Manor."

I hadn't even thought about that. "Oh," I said. "Yes, I see."

Verity swiped a hand under her running nose in a most unladylike manner. "Of course, now I look back, it seems ludicrous. Tommy would never do anything like that. I've just been so tired and worried lately about Dorothy, and with Aldous dying and everything..." She shot me a look that I interpreted as reproachful. "Joan, you refused to tell me who you thought the killer was. I thought that's because you didn't want to tell me because – well, because it was Tommy."

I had to laugh. "V, do you think I would have been as calm as I was if I had thought it was Tommy?"

Verity smiled ruefully. "No. No, of course you wouldn't."

"You noodle," I said, fondly.

Inspector Marks cleared his throat. "This is what happens when people don't talk to one another," he said. "Misunderstandings occur."

"I know that now," said Verity. She sniffed and sat up a little. "It's just that – oh, I don't know. I thought – well, I don't know what I thought."

"All's well that ends well, Miss Hunter," said Inspector Marks.

"Except for poor Aldous," she snapped back.

"Your poor Aldous was a murderer," Inspector Marks said, quite mildly. "It's almost worse that he killed a man because somebody else persuaded him to. I suppose the defence might argue it was a crime of passion but... I wonder."

Verity and I were silent and thoughtful. Then Verity said, tentatively, "Well, he obviously felt some remorse. So much so that he killed himself."

225

"I wonder," Inspector Marks said again. I looked at him sharply.

"What do you mean, Inspector?"

"Just that. I wonder whether he did indeed kill himself. That suicide note was awfully convenient, wasn't it? And half the time, real suicides don't even leave a note."

"What are you suggesting?" I asked, just as my mind leapt along new pathways. I answered myself before he could. "You're saying that Caroline Carpenter could have killed him, aren't you, sir?"

"I don't know." Inspector Marks stared out of the window at the city beyond. "It's a possibility that will be investigated."

He lapsed into silence again and so did we. I was thinking about that suicide note. What had it said? Something like *I find it hard to believe I can carry on living*. Hadn't Tommy said it was on a scrap of paper? That was strange in itself, wasn't it? My mind reconstructed the scrap of paper, fitting it into a full sheet of notepaper, the rest of which was a love letter to Caroline Carpenter. *If your marriage to Sir Nicholas goes ahead, my dearest one, I find it hard to believe I can carry on living...*

Now I *was* being fanciful. I shoved another mental image away, that of Caroline telling Aldous to meet her down by the river, on a dark and shadowed pathway. Had she pointed out something to him in the river, sparkling in the moonlight? And as he leaned forward to see, one push would have done it...

The police would look into it, I told myself firmly. So no more wild imaginings.

The car turned into our street and drew up alongside the pavement. Verity and I pulled our coats more tightly around ourselves. I wondered whether Mrs Watling would be waiting up for me and hoped not. I was too tired to go into explanations.

Inspector Marks opened the door and helped us both out onto the pavement. There was a chill wind blowing that hastened our goodbyes, and overhead a few glimpses of some distant stars were visible, here and there, as the smog blew apart for a few moments.

"Thank you again, ladies," said the inspector. "I'll be in touch."

Verity gave him a quick, wan smile and began to walk down the basement steps. I hesitated, knowing I should follow her but somehow, unable to leave just yet. The inspector and I stood opposite one another for a long moment, shivering in the cold and silent.

"Well, Joan—" He held out his hand to me. I put my gloved one out to shake it. Our eyes met and there was a breathless moment of hush, even over the hubbub of a London night. Slowly the inspector drew the glove from my hand and then clasped my naked palm in his own. His hand was warm and that warmth seemed to spread all the way through me, despite the chill of the night.

"Good night," he said, in quite a different tone to the one he'd just used, when it was Verity and me standing there.

"Goodnight," I said, barely able to get the breath into my lungs to answer him.

He handed me back my glove and waited until I was safely down the steps into the basement. It was only then that I heard the closing of the car door and the sound of the engine as the car drove away.

I almost floated into the kitchen to find it empty of Mrs Watling, thankfully, but with Verity sat slumped at the kitchen table, wearily pulling the hat pins from her hair. Romantic thoughts popped like a soap bubble as I went to sit opposite her. She was so pale and drawn, dark circles like two smudged thumbprints under her eyes, that it was only then I realised the strain she'd been under. I hadn't helped; I hadn't even really noticed, so caught up had I been in solving the case. I resolved then and there to be a better friend.

"Are you all right?"

She gave me a half smile. "Just exhausted, Joan. Mentally and physically." She sighed and said, "I've made up my mind to ask Mrs Anstells for help. With Dorothy, you know. I can't keep it all to myself any longer."

"I think you're wise. Do you want me to come with you?"

Verity shook her head, regretfully. "Thank you, Joanie but no. Forgive me but – but she would see it as an impertinence." She sighed again and said "It's bad enough that I tell her."

I nodded. I understood. "You might find that it doesn't come as quite such a surprise to Mrs Anstells than you think it might. She's not a stupid woman. I'm sure she might have noticed something is amiss."

"I hope you're right." Verity heaved herself to her feet. "I'll go on up now."

"Would you like me to make you a cup of cocoa?"

Verity smiled. "No, thank you, Joanie. But that's kind of you."

For a moment she paused in the doorway, and we smiled at each other and I felt our friendship settle back to how it had been. Inwardly, I breathed a sigh of relief. Then she turned and I listened to her tired feet dragging their way upstairs.

I stayed downstairs for five minutes, heating the milk for my own cup of cocoa and making the finishing touches to preparing the kitchen for tomorrow. By the time I got to our room, Verity was fast asleep, her head half-buried beneath the blankets. She'd left the bedside light on for me.

I got washed and undressed but, despite the cocoa, I didn't believe I'd be able to sleep yet.

There were still too many thoughts and feelings fireworking around in my head. I needed time to put my thoughts in order. I stood for a moment, in the middle of the room, undecided about what to do. Then, letting my feelings guide me, I let my hand reach out for my notebook and my pen. I sat down at the dressing table, tucking a shawl about my shoulders. The blank page lay before me on the surface of the desk, a challenge and a comfort at one and the same time. With one last glance at Verity, sleeping like a baby in her bed, I turned back to the notebook and, dipping the pen into the ink, began to write.

THE END

ENJOYED THIS BOOK? AN HONEST review left at Amazon and Goodreads is always welcome and really important for indie authors. The more reviews an independently published book has, the easier it is to market it and find new readers.

Want some more of Celina Grace's work for free? Subscribers to her mailing list get a free digital copy of Requiem (A Kate Redman Mystery: Book 2), a free digital copy of A Prescription for Death (The Asharton Manor Mysteries Book 2) and a free PDF copy of her short story collection A Blessing from The Obeah Man.

Requiem (A Kate Redman Mystery: Book 2)

WHEN THE BODY OF TROUBLED teenager Elodie Duncan is pulled from the river in Abbeyford, the case is at first assumed to be a straightforward suicide. Detective Sergeant Kate Redman is shocked to discover that she'd met the victim the night before her death, introduced by Kate's younger brother Jay. As the case develops, it becomes clear that Elodie was murdered. A talented young musician, Elodie had been keeping some strange company and was hiding her own dark secrets.

As the list of suspects begin to grow, so do the questions. What is the significance of the painting Elodie modelled for? Who is the man who was seen with her on the night of her death? Is there any connection with another student's death at the exclusive musical college that Elodie attended?

As Kate and her partner Detective Sergeant Mark Olbeck attempt to unravel the mystery, the dark undercurrents of the case threaten those whom Kate holds most dear...

A Prescription for Death (The Asharton Manor Mysteries: Book 2) – a novella

"I HAD A SURGE OF kinship the first time I saw the manor, perhaps because we'd both seen better days."

It is 1947. Asharton Manor, once one of the most beautiful stately homes in the West Country, is now a convalescent home for former soldiers. Escaping the devastation of post-war London is Vivian Holt, who moves to the nearby village and begins to volunteer as a nurse's aide at the manor. Mourning the death of her soldier husband, Vivian finds solace in her new friendship with one of the older patients, Norman Winter, someone who has served his country in both world wars. Slowly, Vivian's heart begins to heal, only to be torn apart when she arrives for work one day to be told that Norman is dead.

It seems a straightforward death, but is it? Why did a particular photograph disappear from Norman's possessions after his death? Who is the sinister figure who keeps following Vivian? Suspicion and doubts begin to grow and when another death occurs, Vivian begins to realise that the war may be over but the real battle is just beginning...

A Blessing from The Obeah Man

DARE YOU READ ON? HORRIFYING, scary, sad and thought-provoking, this short story collection will take you on a macabre journey. In the titular story, a honeymooning couple take a wrong turn on their trip around Barbados. The Mourning After brings you a shivery story from a suicidal teenager. In Freedom Fighter, an unhappy middle-aged man chooses the wrong day to make a bid for freedom, whereas Little Drops of Happiness and Wave Goodbye are tales of darkness from sunny Down Under. Strapping Lass and The Club are for those who prefer, shall we say, a little meat to the story...

JUST GO TO CELINA'S WEBSITE to sign up. It's quick, easy and free. Be the first to be informed of promotions, giveaways, new releases and subscriber-only benefits by subscribing to her (occasional) newsletter.

http://www.celinagrace.com
Twitter: @celina__grace
Facebook: http://www.facebook.
com/authorcelinagrace

Have you read the first Asharton Manor Mystery?

This is the book that introduces Joan and Verity and it's available as a permanently FREE download:

Death at the Manor (The Asharton Manor Mysteries: Book 1)

Please note – this is a novella-length piece of fiction – not a full length novel

IT IS 1929. ASHARTON MANOR stands alone in the middle of a pine forest, once the place where ancient pagan ceremonies were undertaken in honour of the goddess Astarte. The Manor is one of the most beautiful stately homes in the West Country and seems like a palace to Joan Hart, newly arrived from London to take up a servant's position as the head kitchen maid. Getting to grips with her new role and with her fellow workers, Joan is kept busy, but not too busy to notice that the glittering surface of life at the Manor might be hiding some dark secrets. The beautiful and wealthy mistress of the house, Delphine Denford, keeps falling ill but why? Confiding her thoughts to her friend and fellow housemaid, feisty Verity Hunter, Joan is unsure of what exactly is making her uneasy, but then Delphine Denford dies...

Armed only with their own good sense and quick thinking, Joan and Verity must pit their wits against a cunning murderer in order to bring them to justice.

Download Death at the Manor from
Amazon Kindle for free, available now.

Other books by Celina Grace

THE ASHARTON MANOR MYSTERIES

Some old houses have more history than others...

The Asharton Manor Mysteries Boxed Set is a four part series of novellas spanning the twentieth century. Each standalone story (about 20,000 words) uses Asharton Manor as the backdrop to a devious and twisting crime mystery. The boxed set includes the following stories:

DEATH AT THE MANOR

It is 1929. Asharton Manor stands alone in the middle of a pine forest, once the place where ancient pagan ceremonies were undertaken in honour of the goddess Astarte. The Manor is one of the most beautiful stately homes in the West Country and seems like a palace to Joan Hart, newly arrived from London to take up a servant's position as the head kitchen maid. Getting to grips with her new role and with her fellow workers, Joan is kept busy, but not too busy to notice that the glittering surface of life at the Manor might be hiding some dark secrets. The beautiful and wealthy mistress of the house, Delphine Denford, keeps falling ill but why? Confiding her thoughts to her friend and fellow housemaid Verity Hunter, Joan is unsure of what exactly is making her uneasy, but then Delphine Denford dies... Armed only with their own good sense and quick thinking, Joan and Verity must pit their wits against a cunning murderer in order to bring them to justice.

A PRESCRIPTION FOR DEATH

It is 1947. Asharton Manor, once one of the most beautiful stately homes in the West Country, is now a convalescent home for former soldiers. Escaping the devastation of post-war London is Vivian Holt, who moves to the nearby village and begins to volunteer as a nurse's aide at the manor. Mourning the death of her soldier husband, Vivian finds solace in her new friendship with one of the older patients, Norman Winter, someone who has served his country in both world wars. Slowly, Vivian's heart begins to heal, only to be torn apart when she arrives for work one day to be told that Norman is dead. It seems a straightforward death, but is it? Why did a particular photograph disappear from Norman's possessions after his death? Who is the sinister figure who keeps following Vivian? Suspicion and doubts begin to grow and when another death occurs, Vivian begins to realise that the war may be over but the real battle is just beginning...

THE RHYTHM OF MURDER

It is 1973. Eve and Janey, two young university students, are en route to a Bristol commune when they take an unexpected detour to the little village of Midford. Seduced by the roguish charms of a young man who picks them up in the village pub, they are astonished to find themselves at Asharton Manor, now the residence of the very wealthy, very famous, very degenerate Blue Turner, lead singer of rock band Dirty Rumours. The golden summer rolls on, full of sex, drugs and rock and roll, but Eve begins to sense that there may be a sinister side to all the hedonism. And then one day, Janey disappears, seemingly run away... but as Eve begins to question what happened to her friend, she realises that she herself might be in terrible danger...

NUMBER THIRTEEN, MANOR CLOSE

It is 2014. Beatrice and Mike Dunhill are finally moving into a house of their own, Number Thirteen, Manor Close. Part of the brand new Asharton Estate, Number Thirteen is built on the remains of the original Asharton Manor which was destroyed in a fire in 1973. Still struggling a little from the recent death of her mother, Beatrice is happy to finally have a home of her own – until she begins to experience some strange happenings that, try as she might, she can't explain away. Her husband Mike seems unconvinced and only her next door neighbour Mia seems to understand Beatrice's growing fear of her home. Uncertain of her own judgement, Beatrice must confront what lies beneath the beautiful surface of the Asharton Estate. But can she do so without losing her mind – or her life?

Have you met Detective
Sergeant Kate Redman?

THE KATE REDMAN MYSTERIES ARE the
bestselling detective mysteries from Celina Grace,
featuring the flawed but determined female officer
Kate Redman and her pursuit of justice in the West
Country town of Abbeyford.

Hushabye (A Kate Redman Mystery: Book 1)
is the novel that introduces Detective Sergeant Kate
Redman on her first case in Abbeyford. It's available
for free!

**A missing baby. A murdered girl. A case
where everyone has something to hide...**

On the first day of her new job in the West Country, Detective Sergeant Kate Redman finds herself
investigating the kidnapping of Charlie Fullman,
the newborn son of a wealthy entrepreneur and his
trophy wife. It seems a straightforward case... but
as Kate and her fellow officer Mark Olbeck delve
deeper, they uncover murky secrets and multiple
motives for the crime.

Kate finds the case bringing up painful memories of
her own past secrets. As she confronts the truth about
herself, her increasing emotional instability threatens
both her hard-won career success and the possibility
that they will ever find Charlie Fullman alive...

Extra Special Thanks Are Due To My
Wonderful Advance Readers Team…

THESE ARE MY 'SUPER READERS' who are kind
enough to beta read my books, point out my more
ridiculous mistakes, spot any typos that have
slipped past my editor and best of all, write honest
reviews in exchange for advance copies of my work.
Many, many thanks to you all.

If you fancy being an Advance Reader, just drop
me a line at celina@celinagrace.com and I'll add
you to the list. It's completely free, and you can
unsubscribe at any time.

Acknowledgements

MANY THANKS TO ALL THE following splendid souls:

Chris Howard for the brilliant cover designs; Andrea Harding for editing and proofreading; Tammi Lebrecque for virtual assistance; lifelong Schlockers and friends David Hall, Ben Robinson and Alberto Lopez; Ross McConnell for advice on police procedural and for also being a great brother; Kathleen and Pat McConnell, Anthony Alcock, Naomi White, Mo Argyle, Lee Benjamin, Bonnie Wede, Sherry and Amali Stoute, Cheryl Lucas, Georgia Lucas-Going, Steven Lucas, Loletha Stoute and Harry Lucas, Helen Parfect, Helen Watson, Emily Way, Sandy Hall, Kristýna Vosecká, Katie D'Arcy and of course my lovely Chris, Mabel, Jethro and Isaiah.

Printed by Amazon Italia Logistica S.r.l.
Torrazza Piemonte (TO), Italy